dangerous virtues

DANGEROUS VIRTUES

Ana María Moix

Las virtudes peligrosas   Translated & with an
afterword by
Margaret E. W. Jones

University of Nebraska Press : Lincoln & London

Publication of this translation was
assisted by grants from the Spanish
Dirección General del Libro y Biblio-
tecas of the Ministerio de Cultura
and from the Program for Cultural
Cooperation between Spain's Min-
istry of Culture and Education and
United States' Universities.

Originally published as *Las virtudes
peligrosas,* © Ana María Moix, 1985.
Translation and afterword © 1997
by the University of Nebraska Press.

⊗ The paper in this book meets the
minimum requirements of Amer-
ican National Standard for Information Sciences–Permanence of
Paper for Printed Library Materials,
ANSI Z39.48-1984.

Library of Congress Cataloging in Publication Data
Moix, Ana María, 1947–
[Virtudes peligrosas. English]
Dangerous virtues = Las virtudes peligrosas / Ana
María Moix ; translated and with an afterword by
Margaret E. W. Jones. p. cm. – (European women
writers series)
Includes bibliographical references (p.) and index.
ISBN 0-8032-3189-x (cloth : alkaline paper). –
ISBN 0-8032-8237-0 (paperback : alkaline paper)
I. Jones, Margaret E. W., 1938–. II. Title. III. Series.
PQ6663.0345V513 1997 863'.64–dc21 96-37317 CIP

CONTENTS

Acknowledgments: Several people deserve recognition for their contributions to this translation: Bonnie Cox, for her careful reading of the manuscript; Marta Roller, for her help with questions about Spanish language and children's rhymes; and Carol Maier, for her expertise in the theory and practice of translation. And to Joseph R. Jones, the ideal reader and critic, my gratitude for his knowledge, helpful suggestions, and encouragement.

d a n g e r o u s   v i r t u e s

For Madol Coma and Mariano de la Cruz

For Rosa Sender

DANGEROUS VIRTUES

No, Alice, if you think about it and you are honest about what you remember, you will admit the truth: you never did see the elderly woman's eyes. Show the film our senses make—involuntarily in most cases—when they establish their not always voluntary contact with reality; have your mental projector rewind that film to the point where the protagonist—you, Alice—was ten or twelve, and watch the same sequence over and over, see yourself dressed in your school uniform, breathless, hair tousled, as you entered the elderly woman's apartment at five in the afternoon, all set to begin the hour of reading.

The light in the garden would be fading on the windowpanes covered with long, embroidered, white curtains—solitary dancers prompted by the slight breeze to a slow imitation of a waltz; and the face of the old woman, sitting in her chair, would turn toward you, just as you appeared in the doorway. From there you would make out the upright, slim figure always dressed in blue and gray silk, the long neck turning a pale, nacreous face toward you, the thin, perfect lips parted in a friendly smile; a well-shaped nose; a head of elegant proportions framed by bluish, always slightly wavy hair. In the middle of that snowy white and rosy oval, dark glasses hid eyes that—remember this, Alice— you had a strange feeling were staring at you not only when she greeted you (raising one hand slightly while keeping the other one, which you never saw tremble, on the knob of her cane) but during the entire time that you were reading.

Sitting in the chair next to the window, apparently peaceful and calm (let's be aware, from now on, that the term *apparently* applies to all the details and scenes that pass through your mind, no matter how insignificant they may seem and perhaps may be), the motionless figure received you, surrounded by a silence whose solemn command of the room was defied only by the insubordinate notes of the birds' intermittent song and the willow's foliage in the wind in the garden; nor was there the least reason not to believe that she had been in exactly the same position for a long time, perhaps hours, before your arrival. It is easy to picture her, to suppose that she was that way. Supposing is a frivolous ability, and we all have it.

And yet, after you had greeted the concierge and gardener at the gate, and the maid who opened the door for you, and Miss S., who came out to meet you and warn you in a low voice, *don't read to madame too long; after you leave, at night, she suffers from bad headaches,* as you were climbing the long flight of stairs to the second floor, leaving below the mansion's only inhabitants, what did you think was making the heavy sound that came from the floor above, the very place to which you were going, or the rapid, light footsteps? No, you never stopped to wonder, Alice. And when you opened the door to the elderly woman's rooms, after knocking and hearing the cordial *come in,* the semi-invalid, sightless woman would be sitting next to the window, in her lap the ribbons, bows, wreaths of tulle and flowers, and lace that, almost daily, she would give you during the game—amusing to you—the rite, both incomprehensible and indecipherable when you reflected on it later, that consisted, once the reading was over, of your approaching the elderly woman in obedience to her pleasant but firm summons—remember, there was a firmness, an imperious command in her words, although they were softened by her warm voice when she said, *come here, my dear, I have a surprise for you.* With shaking hands she groped at the air before touching your body lightly with her long, thin fingers, fumbling at your waist with her slender hands in order to untie the bow that, in identical circumstances, the other woman, who was also elderly and in whose house you likewise read, had given you the day before, and replace it with a different one. But her hands would not stop shaking as she caressed your hair and pulled it back with gold barrettes that replaced the ones put there, the day before, by the other elderly woman. Each of the women kept the gifts bestowed on your body by the other, and by a curious coincidence, they were identical, which you thought would prevent either of them from complaining when she saw her offerings replaced, although, because they were sightless, as their dark glasses and behavior indicated, they would hardly have been able to notice it.

But no, Alice, no, you were not aware of the elderly woman's shaking hands as she ran them over your hair, your waist, the cuffs of the sleeve on your arm, or the greedy way she clasped the articles and objects that she removed from you, or the light in her eyes that, hidden by the glasses, you never saw. In an excited voice, which you assumed was peculiar to advanced age, elated with pleasure (*old women are happy when they give gifts,* she used to say to you), she would tell you, as she continued to array you, about the life of the people whose portraits covered the walls of the room, which was austere in contrast with the rest of the luxurious house—the bed, a wardrobe whose mirrors you noticed were always covered with black veils, and a writing desk: the portrait of a tall, robust man with a heavy white mustache, dressed in a military uniform with a sash and various medals displayed on his chest—the general, the great strategist, the husband of the elderly woman, who had died many years ago under the merciless desert sun, a victim of insanity, it was said. Beside that portrait, the picture of an elegant young man, corpulent like the unfortunate general, but with the elderly woman's enchanting smile: her son, Rudolph, whose scientific research took him far away to live in a remote place in North Africa.

Two canvases hanging opposite one another on parallel walls portrayed two figures of women of extraordinary beauty. Dressed in low-cut white gowns, both women radiated a subtle mixture of haughtiness, pride, peace, and serenity, and one felt unsettled—did you feel that way too? remember—by the urgency of the search in their penetrating, wounding gazes that were expectant but also tinged with melancholy and resignation. Yes, those two young women, whom the elderly woman never mentioned, reminded you of someone. On one occasion only, she whispered a weak *they died*, turning her dark glasses toward the wardrobe mirrors covered with black veils.

You didn't even wonder, my dear Alice, why mirrors had terrified the elderly woman for years, or why, according to remarks you heard Miss S. and the maid make, she had ordered them covered forever, since, being blind, she could see neither them nor herself in them. Perhaps the order dated from a time before she lost her sight, an accident never mentioned in any way by the elderly woman or any other inhabitant of the house. Nor did you notice the only discordant note in the meticulous order not only in the old woman's room but in the whole house: her bed usually seemed askew, breaking the symmetry it was surely supposed to have with the wall and the wardrobe, and in addition, the bedspread itself was uneven. The noises you heard when you were climbing the stairs, which seemed to be produced by someone dragging a very heavy object, and the hurried footsteps came from that room; yes, now that you are making an effort to remember, you discover that, on more than one occasion, you associated the noise with the dislocated bed, but it was a question of a vague association born spontaneously in your mind, with none of the intentionality that would necessarily generate a cause or solution. Nothing there led you to suspect mysterious acts or phenomena, and the only thing that piqued your fleeting and rather playful curiosity was the coincidence that both elderly women for whom you used to read in the afternoons had a desire to comb your hair, give you bows, flower wreaths, or bracelets, a desire attributable to the kindness of the two women and also to their generosity.

Nevertheless, your curiosity about the behavior of the elderly woman would disappear immediately, wiped out by the only thing that really intrigued you in that room, which was the presence of two canvases, executed by the same painter to judge by the identical signature on each, of the two young, extraordinarily beautiful women. *They died*, the elderly woman had said, riveting her dark glasses on the black veils of the wardrobe mirrors. But the two painted faces recalled faces of familiar people in your daily life, and the initials of one of the two young women, engraved on the gilded frame of the painting, were the same as those of the elderly woman, inscribed in her books and on the objects on her dressing table.

The artist who painted them knew how to express with his brushes the mystery that the deceased strategist-general, during the last painful years of his life, and you, Alice, never penetrated. It was not the unquestionable beauty of the two slim bodies, their sensual shapes contrasting with a distant and cold bearing, the delicate, soft line of neck and shoulders, the fleshy, warm lips, the silky hair, one blond, the other darker; your attention was not attracted by the beauty of the two women or by their mixture of pride and serenity, of haughtiness and curious tenderness. Their gaze was the source of your uneasiness. With the canvases facing one another, the painter seemed to have captured the women in the very act of looking at each other. The eyes of one were riveted on those of the other, and vice versa; they possessed each other urgently and, at the same time, with the placidity of the eternal. *They died,* the elderly woman murmured one afternoon, turning her dark glasses toward the black veils that covered the mirrors. But first — did you notice? — first, Alice, yes, now you do remember, she looked up, and her dark glasses turned toward one canvas and then toward the other. That very afternoon, she had you read: *He who possesses the gift of beauty dies young, if he wishes to die beautiful. Others will possess that beauty in him, but he will struggle in a world of inferior forms, possessing only himself or, even worse, his equal, should he find him in his path. Then both suffer a sad fate, that of never separating, for after the exultant period of elation, when the beauty of one is reflected in the beauty of the other — reciprocal mirrors of charm and grace — then this very indissolubility condemns them eventually to reproach each other for the deterioration wrought in them by the years — sickness, old age, and death — simply because they display themselves to each other, or, what amounts to the same thing, contemplate each other. Only equals who cease to exist for the world of corruptible forms at the moment when they enjoy full possession of their beauty, before the onset of decrepitude has damaged them, will remain eternally beautiful in the immutable mirror that each has been for the other.*

They died, she whispered, not to you, Alice, but to the black veils on the mirrors. Nevertheless, not even then did you understand. Neither did the deceased strategist-general, dead for more than thirty years, respected at Court for his military talents, favored by His Majesty, the nobility, and the highest dignitaries for his victorious campaigns in the colonies, admired for his valor, chivalry, and because he was the husband of one of the most beautiful women in the country. *But he didn't understand,* the elderly woman would comment when you, Alice, asked questions about the general, curious about the extravagant story according to which the brilliant military strategist fell prey, in the colonies, to a strange madness that swept him to his death. Yes, it was true, and during the final months preceding the unfortunate outcome, alarm had already spread through the military staff because of reports received in the strategist-general's own handwriting, in which he jumbled incidents from the field campaigns with the deranged account of curious and unconfirmed events that had occurred in his married life.

Yes, the brilliant, corpulent strategist was a romantic.

You held the general's manuscripts in your hands, Alice. Did you read them? Did you read how passionately he describes his return home, after five years of barely uninterrupted action in the colonies, to be once again with his adored young wife and his little Rudolph? For a time, a series of parties took place at Court and at the mansion of the general, who was always accompanied by his resplendent wife. Did she ever fail to accompany him? Did she replace her husband's company with another man's? No, never. They separated only when they attended the opera, and this was a long-standing arrangement between them, something she desired, which she explained with the sincerity and naturalness of a lady, and which he respected with the courtesy and discretion characteristic of a gentleman. As a lover of opera, she preferred to enjoy the performance (the *beauty,* she always specified) alone, without the obligatory companionship imposed by social demands.

Yes, Alice, the dates of the general's manuscripts, as well as the information therein, are not contradictory, although written down by an already feverish mind: the operatic evening took place not long after the return of the general, who witnessed the performance from the royal box.

Music tames the savage beast, but this was not exactly the case with the brilliant strategist, who possessed, even though he was a man devoted from youth, by vocation and training, to military life, a certain sensitivity that permitted him to enjoy the pleasures of music and some other arts like oratory and poetry, although not to the degree that it filled him completely, transporting him and monopolizing his entire faculty of thought; part of his mind remained free and ready to stroll among those objects that attracted his attention. First he recalled certain comments of an ambassador with whom he had started a conversation before the performance began; then he noticed His Majesty's healthy appearance; some matter not yet settled in the colonies crossed his mind; and, standing next to His Majesty, while the movements of his hand, resting on the back of the august chair, unconsciously followed the notes of the music, he observed out of the corner of his eye the occupants of the neighboring boxes or glanced over the orchestra circle and upper galleries of the theater, packed during that gala performance. He was also wearing his full-dress uniform, its breast crossed with the honorific sash, embellished with medals whose number and rank had recently been increased after five years of service. After five years in the colonies, however, he had to make a great effort to concentrate on the plot unfolding on stage with its Germanic heroes; and when you add the many meetings with former comrades to his aforementioned feeling of disengagement, you will understand, Alice, the reasons for the general's scattered thoughts and inability to follow the development of the music and plot. He looked through his opera glasses toward the stage in a final attempt to take an interest in the performance by taking pleasure in the face and bearing of some of the artists; but the vociferating mouths and grimaces made him smile, and giving up the effort, he unconsciously turned his opera glasses toward his wife's box.

There she was, resplendent in her low-cut white dress, conspicuous in the general semidarkness, sitting up straight in her seat, majestic, one hand resting in her lap and the other, raised, holding the opera glasses in the direction of—no, not the stage—the box exactly opposite hers. Women are so very curious, smiled the brilliant strategist stroking his recently graying mustache. Whom could his wife be so curious about? And after a long while, he looked at her again.

Yes, Alice, she was in the same position, looking through her opera glasses, and the general's glasses followed their direction until he discovered that his wife's glasses were trained steadily on the figure of a woman, also dressed in white, the solitary occupant of the box opposite that of his wife, on whom the unknown woman was focusing her opera glasses at the same time. Five, ten, twenty, more than thirty minutes went by; a dull irritation upset the general's mind, and his hand, which had directed the most difficult battles, planned the most astute attacks, and held all kinds of weapons, began to ache as for more than half an hour it stiffly gripped the opera glasses with which he watched first his wife and then the unknown woman contemplate each other in utter delight, with no signs of fatigue. No, the general did not know whether the impious, brutal reverberation in his head was the hammering notes of Wagner or the throbbing of his own heart. His rapid breathing seemed like a stagnant wind in which a sickening vortex swirled, the red velvet of the walls and seats, the scarlet of the uniforms around him, merged with the darkness at the back of the stall and the thousand green, blue, violet, and gold tints of the stage set; and standing out all the while in this relentless multicolored kaleidoscope, were the two white figures, the two women joined by the ferrous but invisible prolongation of their respective glances through the opera glasses focused constantly in each other's direction, generating a bond that was exclusively theirs, a bond that was soft and tender but endowed with the firmness and certainty of something that had already come to pass, a bond that like a whiplash cut him to the quick. There, standing next to His Majesty, he felt the torture of the strange sharp weapon created by the two women as they looked at each other face to face; he sensed a carnal warmth cross the orchestra from box to box; as they looked at each other, they were creating a monster that would protect them; they were invulnerable to everything, but that monster would hurl itself on him, take him far away from the range of that reciprocal gaze, and pitilessly tear at him until it defeated him.

It was then, Alice, that he shuddered, quivering, shaken by rage and pain. Noting this, His Majesty asked, *Is something the matter, General?* Pale and sweating, he murmured a weak, faltering, *It is only the sound of Wagner's trumpets, sire.* A red cloud blinded his eyes; it was impossible for him to decide whether his brief explanation was smashing against the scarlet silks of the presidential box or against the desert sun, implacable above his campaign tent for years. It was the sun that wounded him cruelly; it burned his eyes, parched his throat, under the red velvet that covered the walls and floor of the theater; when dimmed in the chandelier in the high dome, its temporary eclipse was prolonged by hundreds of precious crystal drops; when it shone, how brightly it glinted on the necklaces in the décolletage of his wife's dress and in the décolletage of the unknown woman. It burned.

He clenched his jaw rigidly, Alice, and the blood boiled in his veins, about to burst. But during his military campaigns, the strategist-general had always conquered the sun; he bore it or he used it to conquer the enemy. Why not now? he wondered. The sun would come out, it would light up in the gigantic lamp in the dome, in the hundreds of lamps scattered about the theater; its fierce brilliance, multiplied as it was reflected in the mirrors, in the women's jewels, and in the gold of the ornaments in the house, would annihilate the monster, the communion borne from opera glass to opera glass between the two women dressed in white. Yes, when the act was over, after a few seconds, the sudden illumination of the room would shatter the long, invisible embrace of those powerful gazes; the applause would silence the mute, affectionate dialogue at a distance, from box to box; the murmur of greetings between ladies and gentlemen, the brush of silk against uniform, the creaking of seats temporarily vacated, the noise of bodies rising from their chairs — all would help to break, to destroy, to sever that long, extended gaze that had become tactile and that consumed him from within. Lively social activity, again under way, would disturb the firmness and tranquillity of the two women's immobile expressions. In that burst of light, it would be impossible for those two hands to continue impassively to hold high the opera glasses trained on each other like two beacons submerged in an ocean. There was only one secret pleasure that could calm the anger contained in the great strategist's breast: his observation, through his own opera glasses, of defeat on the faces of the two women when, as the curtain fell, darkness must cease to protect the secret union, must give way to the light that would vaporize that private floating island created by the two of them. With what delight he would witness how the revival of public social life would force those hands down and relegate them to the women's laps or to the arm of the chair, while their cunning extensions, the opera glasses, would lie as if blind on the adjoining seat.

Nevertheless, the strategist-general would not witness the longed-for defeat. Just moments before the lights went on, the gloved hands and the two women dressed in white disappeared from their boxes: as if by mutual agreement, as if the action were part of a ritual performed many times over, they stopped looking at each other, obeying no outward command.

The strategist-general never lost his sangfroid and organizational power under even worse conditions, and, while he returned greetings, comments, compliments, and congratulations from the royal entourage and those who came to the vestibule of the august box, he put all his craftiness to work and mobilized every man at his disposal to spread a net of surveillance between his wife's box and that of the other woman. In which of the two boxes would they meet? Or in which corner of the theater? Perhaps they would limit themselves to starting a conversation as their paths crossed or to strolling together through the halls, he thought, incapable of controlling the throbbing inside that breast decorated with the honorific sash and various medals, although it also harbored a steely pain and the sharp presentiment that, as he ordered his men to look into a matter that was disagreeable but not difficult to clear up, he was taking the first step toward the investigation of *something* whose outcome would be dark and mysterious. Meanwhile, His Majesty rested a friendly hand on his stiff shoulder and affably commented, *Wouldn't such intense emotion at the sound of Wagner's trumpets indicate that you are worn out? You are pale, General. Perhaps, without realizing it, the crown is taking advantage of our distinguished general's service in the colonies? What do you think, Marshal? Are our colonies worth the exhaustion of men as valuable as the general?*

From what a distance he heard the kind offer proposed by His Majesty, who raised a glass of champagne along with those accompanying him: the sovereign voice granting him a generous leave, the murmurs and faint laughter in the vestibule growing muffled as he heard his wife's words, brought back by his memory; *how happy I would be to have a box at my disposal, to be able to attend the performances without the boring companionship required by protocol; I have wanted this for so long!*

When did she ask him? Before his last campaign? Before, long before. Five, seven, almost ten years before, when Rudolph was born. Almost ten years wanting to be alone in the box, opposite that of . . . Who could it be? When the intermission was over, his men would tell him. He longed to return home and, instead of wishing his wife goodnight, to reproach her with everything his men would have confided to him. With a woman! And at the opera, the most public place in the capital! Rumors and jokes must have circulated through the Court, the palace, the army, throughout the whole city, the whole country; they would have reached every corner except the colonies. How was it possible that he had never suspected—he, the great, the crafty fox of His Majesty's armies. He smiled; he heard his own voice joining in with the marshal's comments, *opera is démodé, my dear General, there are few minds capable of inventing new amusements;* nevertheless, he pictured himself abandoning such illustrious company with a brusque gesture, leaving the royal box abruptly, running through the halls of the theater, breaking into the vestibule of the box where they . . . No, it would be better to restrain himself and wait until later that night, with the proof in hand.

A dizzy spell accompanied the feeling of confusion that followed the brief conversation with his men: his wife had not left the vestibule of her box during the intermission, nor did anyone come to it; neither had the other woman, about whom he requested information, left hers, nor had she received any visitor. When asked, all the employees concurred that both women attended the opera performances regularly, always alone, and they never received guests in their boxes.

When the lights were lowered again, however, and the musical movements of the second act began, the women, in their white dresses, sat down in their facing boxes, and the opera glasses of one sought those of the other without hesitating, Alice, without first glancing at the stage or at any part of the rest of the house, and they remained fixed on each other for the entire performance.

He didn't understand, murmured the elderly woman, referring to the deceased general as she carefully combed your hair and pushed back her dark glasses with an apprehensive gesture, as if afraid that someone (only you, Alice, were in the room) might pull them off. Did the idea of doing that ever tempt you? Perhaps after you discovered Rudolph's studio? The elderly woman never confided to you that the first, the real vocation of her son was painting; repentant, he abandoned this vocation and career in a state of desolation and confusion after the curse on him uttered by his father, the strategist-general, and the latter's subsequent death.

He didn't understand, lamented the elderly woman. That operatic evening marked a brusque change in the general's character. Having accepted the leave granted by His Majesty, with no set time for rejoining the army—a leave that until then he had refused time and again—the general's character deteriorated; one minute he seemed bitter and silent, the next excessively happy and jovial, never consistent with the prevailing mood of others, responding only to his own feeling: such egotistical behavior thus ruined his reputation for courtliness.

Although it is true that he began to act in this discourteous way deliberately and only in the presence of his wife, as vengeance for her nights at the opera—which he could neither oppose by using logic nor reprove forcefully by specifying facts and concrete evidence (those facts, although impossible to prove and thus impossible to brandish as concrete, forever destroyed his placid, tranquil sentimentality, binding him to doubt, to jealousy, to anxiety and anguish; and, when he felt their pain and when their incorporeal, phantasmal nature prevented him from identifying them by name, they became a cause of resentment and unjustifiable rudeness toward all close to him)—little by little, such emotional outbursts, voluntary at first, became uncontrollable even for him, since he did not submit them to liberal doses of corrective measures; at times, this unrestraint was reason enough for his increasingly rash behavior.

Detached and uninterested in the feelings of others, more and more indifferent and inattentive to their struggles, worries, triumphs, or happiness, the general was immersed only in his own worries; his state of mind responded solely to the course of the elements that produced it. And, to tell the truth, the general's worries were few—only one to be exact: his wife. His country property was in the hands of an administrator, as it had been during the times he was away, so aside from a few—ever more infrequent—hours allotted to physical exercise and chess games with the few former compeers whose long friendship and undying comradeship enabled them to put up with his inopportune and frequently intolerable company, the general spent most of his time absorbed in his wife, the only person with whom he continued behaving, curiously enough, with the same refinement, good breeding, and courtliness as before, although he did introduce one variation into his relationship with her: long silences. For her part, in no way had she changed her behavior toward the general since they had married ten years before. And if her gaze seemed abstracted, and her gestures and expression somewhat melancholy (although, beginning with the night at the opera, such states were a cause for alarm and suspicion for the general, irritated that he could not follow her thoughts), he did not reproach her at all, because after the initial, instinctive, secret vexation, he realized that even when he had first known her she had been given to discreet nostalgia.

No wound on the battlefield caused him as much pain as he felt when he would return home alone, shaking uncontrollably, wondering how it was possible not to bleed, the arrows of pain and confusion piercing the deepest part of his breast, after going out secretly to follow his wife through the city and discovering her long, peaceful strolls along one of the avenues of the park, under the linden trees, placidly keeping pace with the other woman on the other side of the avenue. Wearing dresses of the same color, both walked slowly, separated by the road, not speaking to each other, but wrapped in a happiness and security that separated them from all other human beings and, of course, from him. They took pleasure in this. They walked for hours and hours without conversing or meeting, and with no farewell, they separated with the same naturalness that had characterized their meeting.

A dull anger consumed him. He would have wished a thousand times over for the rivalry of a lover rather than that indestructible, demonic alliance; a thousand times over, someone he could struggle with, shout at, conquer, no matter whether he lost or died; anything would be a thousand times preferable to the constant mockery and humiliation of months, at first, and,

later, years of two presences who met unexpectedly, then separated, exchanging only their gazes, always dressed in the same
color, endowed not only with extraordinary beauty but also
with the superiority granted by the gift of knowing they would
always be together, no matter where they might be. In time, the
cruel, heartrending pangs of jealousy gave way to the no less
torturous ones of incomprehension, and those of incomprehension to those of envy of the indissoluble union that he perceived between the two. It wrapped them in an untouchable
and invulnerable aura that set them apart from other mortals as
they walked through the park or along the streets, sat in church
or on a bench on the avenue, staring into each other's eyes: they
felt it, they possessed it, *they were* this union and this alone. It
was useless to try to discover what means they used to arrange
meetings or to communicate with each other. He watched the
mail, the servants, all modes of communication; he was present
at the appointments of his wife with the seamstress, with the
dressmaker, with the hairdresser, with any possible messenger;
he accompanied her to the stores and shops of the city, he spied
on her conversations with friends and family members . . .

After he had suffered the torment of jealousy, humiliation,
and incomprehension for years, fear settled into his brain. He
became accustomed to seeing them together, to following secretly the strolls of those two women about whose strange adventure he could never tell anyone, any sane human being.
Powerful, distinctive, they scourged the mediocrity surrounding them; defiant, in the cold light of day, they displayed a
union founded on a mystery that no one would ever be able to
decipher. Seated opposite each other on a bench on the avenue,
in sunshine, in rain, wind, or soft breeze, they contemplated
each other for hours. Did they communicate, perhaps through
thought? Never, never would he manage to find out. His almost
deranged reason beat against clouds of extravagant ideas, and
if he intercepted their gazes, he felt as if whips were lashing
him mercilessly, again and again, to separate him from the two
women.

No, Alice, no. When the exhausted, ailing general—prey at first only to nighttime terrors and later, also, to daytime terrors, during which the gaze held by the two women turned into a slimy, cruel snake that coiled around his neck, not to the point of strangulation but keeping him in a continual state of asphyxia—decided, on medical advice, to retire for a period of time to his house in the country, he did not ask his wife to accompany him, surely fearing the possibility of her refusal, since she would not want to give up her unusual meetings, a refusal that would increase his desperation. Nevertheless, it was she who decided to join him on that restful sojourn in the country before the death of the strategist-general, for whom his wife's horseback rides, the first thing in the morning, almost at dawn, were nothing new because he knew that she had enjoyed those rides from the first time he brought her with him to that lush green estate, and throughout many visits there, she never failed to ride, although, as the general observed on this last trip, she did not devote as much time to the rides.

Was it mere curiosity—as he repeated to himself when he ordered his horse to be readied—or an unhealthy desire to confirm a dark, terrible presentiment with his own eyes? He was forced to dismount and hide behind a large rock for shelter as he wept. Far from the city, under the blue sky still stained with the pink striations of dawn, they rode in green riding habits paler than the green of the fields; at first they kept pace rhythmically, next they began a fast trot, then they dismounted without speaking to each other and walked together toward the horizon.

When he returned, depressed, with a vacant stare, after confirming from a servant the recent arrival of new owners on the neighboring estate, he gave up his custom of carrying out exhaustive inquiries and decided not to leave the house again. At most, he would take the sun in the garden watching Rudolph reproduce the surrounding nature on canvas.

I don't know, Alice, if it could have been avoided. But yes, it was there, in the country house, that Rudolph painted his mother's portrait. Although young—he may not even have been twenty at that time—he had already painted the portrait of several well-known ladies in the city with notable skill and success. There, in the family residence, the scene that the general described and inserted into a military report probably took place: since his wife's face was singularly luminous when she returned from her daily ride, and since he was feeling rather weak and melancholy, he asked her to pose in white for their son; as if seized by the presentiment that inevitable and total disaster was imminent, he wanted Rudolph to reproduce his mother's beauty on canvas, his real reason that he might contemplate his wife while she posed, contemplate her openly, without the suspicious scrutiny of the ill-disguised and furtive looks he had directed toward her for years now as he tried to discover in her face some hidden secret. Once his request was accepted with delight by mother and son, the general immediately repented of his wish: full of horror, overcome by a panic that increased by the minute, he saw how his son captured—incredibly, remarkably—his mother's gaze, that gaze, the very one, the one that he, the general, feared and knew as his executioner. But the matter was irreversible; it was already too late to interrupt the execution of the painting, to restrain Rudolph's feverish inspiration, and neither mother nor son listened to the general's laments, orders, or entreaties.

Yes, Alice, that was the house in which Rudolph painted his mother, that house, the old family estate of the general who, with contorted face and inhuman cries, ordered them to brick up the doors and windows and build a fire around it so the mansion would be fuel for the blaze, so not a trace of it should remain after the last turbulent night before the family's return to the city.

Was the brightness of the full moon through the bedroom windows the cause of his waking in the middle of the night, or the noise of footsteps on the upper floor? Whatever the reason for his insomnia, he first felt discomfort, then danger, as if a mysterious, repugnant presence were spying on his movements, in search of the right moment to stab him in the back; he even felt the cold proximity of steel on his flesh while an invisible iron force squeezed his throat and hampered his breathing. Not daring to move, shaken by initial panic, he then reacted and, determined to find out the truth at last, revolver in hand, he climbed to the upper floor from where the noctambulant's footsteps were coming. His shoulders were covered by a fur coat, and he could not believe it: the icy, hurricane-like night wind penetrated the room through wide-open windows and whipped his wife's light nightgown as, half-naked in the light of the full moon, she defied the bleak weather in the gallery overlooking the woods that surrounded the house. Impassive, motionless, she stared at a point in the woods without noticing behind her the presence of the general, whose revolver aimed at the target (the object of his wife's contemplation, a woman on horseback, in the trees, looking toward the house) and he fired once, several times, until he emptied the magazine of the revolver.

It was he, Alice, who cried out as he fired the shots, seized with terror and desperation, and even later, after throwing the fatal weapon into the dark garden and writhing on the floor, when he tried with both hands to free himself from something that seemed to throttle him and begged forgiveness of his wife who, disconcerted by the general's behavior but with a calm, steady voice—the way she usually spoke to her husband during the last years, when he showed signs of absurd reactions produced by a certain disorder she attributed to the long, hard sojourns in the colonies—asked, *Is something the matter, my dear? Are you ill?* At the touch of his wife's hands, warm in spite of having remained for hours exposed to the icy night winds, he fainted.

As the servant bid them goodbye on the following morning, after the general's sudden decision to return to the city and to raze the house, he commented on the discovery of a horse that had died from bullet wounds in the woods near the house. Pale and shaking, with wild, sunken eyes, the general insisted, before leaving, on carrying out a meticulous search of the woods to ascertain whether any more dead or wounded were lying there. *Only the horse, General,* announced the servant as the result of the search, *it must have run away from the stables on the neighboring estate, frightened by last night's terrible storm, and a traveler killed it. Frightened horses are usually dangerous.*

The unknown woman had escaped. The general could not understand how, but he gave up pursuing the matter, sunken into an existence devoted to reflections that, now having admitted defeat and glimpsed the shadows of madness, he knew would clarify nothing for him about that remarkable story, begun ten years earlier in the opera house, by which he let himself be absorbed in so destructive a way that it removed him from the social and political life of his country and had plunged him into sickness, decline, and obsession.

After his return to the city, he began what in his military reports he called *a final attempt at survival.* With a supreme effort of will and sacrifice, he gave up following his wife when she left home. Certain that she was going to meet the other woman, the general overcame his inclination to spy on them, and when the temptation was about to overcome him, the memory of the two women's gaze transformed into a revolting, foul snake coiled around his own neck came to his aid. Taciturn but more affable, with the unmistakable expression typical of those who have suffered—or are suffering—a deep, incurable wound, pathetically desirous of reestablishing human contact with those who were his friends and comrades, he reopened his salons with the help of his wife, solicitous, perfect, and beautiful as she had never failed to be, and of Rudolph, happy, cordial, heir to his mother's beauty and to the nobility of spirit that formerly characterized his father, from whom only one point of contention separated him, a cause of friction and mutual misunderstandings: the young man's vocation for painting, an art he was determined not to renounce because his work was considered so brilliant and exceptional that, in spite of his youth, it had already gained a certain fame and position for him.

Gradually, the general avoided confronting the only two causes that could renew his blind desperation and hard combat in the sharp claws of the demon of the unknown: his son's career and the sight of the portrait Rudolph had painted of his mother, a canvas admired by all who visited the house but which the general, since his return from the country, refused to look at again, not even allowing himself to remain too long, or alone, in the room where it was hanging. Having conquered to a certain degree these two obsessions, the general participated again in the social life of the city; he renewed contact with old comrades; he spent hours in physical exercise both for pleasure and in case the crown should need his services in the future; he threw himself into the game of chess with a passion; he took an interest in new inventions for warfare, and although the secret and uninterrupted alliance of the two women was present in his mind, he considered the irremediable, dark matter with resignation, which allowed him to enjoy moments of tranquillity and even of excellent humor.

No, Alice, the general's well-being, and that of his home, did not—as you know—last. He wrote, *as soon as I entered the drawing room I saw the horrible snake; it pounced on me and coiled around my neck.* But it did not happen that way; the truth is that it took quite a while for him to discover the presence of the second portrait. Staring at his interlocutor, or at his cup—as he usually did when they insisted on serving tea in the room where the portrait of his wife was hanging, to avoid seeing it—he could not help raising his head and eyes in an instinctive movement when he heard someone comment, *marvelous, Rudolph, truly extraordinary; the portrait of this woman is as perfect as your mother's,* and when he saw her, when he saw the two of them, his teacup fell from his hands onto the carpet. Rudolph's explanation to his interlocutor came from far away, *I don't know who she is, but she truly possesses an exceptional beauty; no, this is not a painter's exaggeration. She appeared in my studio, commissioned the portrait for which she paid in advance, and to this moment, she has shown no interest in it. I hung it here because, I don't know why, it seems to complement the other one: they are both wearing the same white dress, both expressions* . . . A terrible cry broke from the general's throat, and with flushed, contorted face, he looked first at the portrait of his wife, then at the painting recently hung directly across on the opposite wall: the one of his wife and the one of the other woman. From both canvases they stared at each other, generating a current that shook him from his head to the tip of his toes. They contemplated each other, creating a world inhabited by them alone and ruled by them alone, as they did from their respective boxes at the opera, during their strolls through the park, the streets, or in the country at dawn, as they managed to do even during stormy nights in full moon, one half-naked on the roof terrace, the other riding through the woods. No, Alice, the general could not bear the *presence* of those stares in his own house, those gazes captured on the canvases by his own son; they had become a reality under the roof of his own home from which, implacably, they expelled him.

To the astonishment of those present, red with anger and seized with strange convulsions, the general yanked off his foulard and shirt collar with both hands as he uttered cries of pain, roared insults at his son, cursed invisible snakes, and ran out of the room and the house, never to return. He rejoined the army in the colonies and after several months he died of asphyxia, according to the official communiqué. His comrades from that period stated that the general suffered from frequent nightmares in which he was attacked and strangled by a monstrous reptile—according to what he shouted in his sleep. Taken to the hospital for an obligatory rest cure, he was found dead one morning, hanging from the window of his room, swinging on the outer facade of the building, his body whipped by the hurricane-like wind that had been raging that night on the desert.

No, Alice, the blindness of the elderly woman you read to in the afternoons was not caused by the general in an attack of anger and revenge. The story is not true—although it caused a great deal of commentary—in its account of how the brilliant strategist tore out his wife's eyes after he discovered the second woman's portrait before he left for the colonies. I know, Alice, because I was in the house that afternoon.

Although it is true that his wife's confinement to the rooms where you visit her every other afternoon dates approximately from the time of the general's unhappy end, he caused it neither with any violent action nor with his death, *which will overtake me without allowing me time to uncover the mystery,* as he wrote in his last military report. A mystery that you, Alice, began to understand intuitively when you detected one of the many lies told by the elderly woman in reply to your questions while she was placing ribbons and bows around your waist or combing your hair. Yes, you do remember: referring to Rudolph, whose photograph you were looking at, she explained that his scientific research obliged him to live in a remote spot in North Africa. Nevertheless, in the other house, in the rooms of the other woman to whom you would read, who was also elderly, almost invalid, and sightless, as you searched through papers and notebooks in a bureau drawer for a book of poems requested by the old woman, you found a yellowing photograph, a reproduction of the image of a young man (*a great artist,* explained the old woman, *who painted my portrait many years ago*) who looked exactly like Rudolph, in the picture hanging in the room of the other elderly woman who, when you questioned her again, since you were now suspicious and wanted to see whether she contradicted herself, repeated to you that her son devoted himself to research. Was it at that time when you began to have doubts about everything the elderly woman told you: about Rudolph's activities, about the death of the women in the paintings, about the natural death of the strategist-general, about everything except her blindness?

Secretly and without permission, you dared to enter rooms to which you were not allowed access. Don't misrepresent the reasons for your curiosity now, because your mind is capable of greater and deeper reflection. No, Alice, now that you are in possession of information that is arranged, more or less, in some order, do not pretend retrospectively that you had, in the past, a suspicion you did not have; do not pretend you entered the forbidden rooms in search of proof that would unmask the elderly woman. No, be honest as you remember it: wondering whether art or research was Rudolph's real profession, you decided it was the second, and when you dared to enter rooms to which no one called you, you did it driven only by the desire to discover paintings as beautiful as those of the two women hanging on the walls of the old woman's room. In one wing, on the top floor of the house, you found what in other times must have been Rudolph's studio. Yes. But no painting satisfied your curiosity.

From inside my room, I heard your footsteps and heard how you opened the door slowly, timidly, thus giving me time to hide. I was concealed behind a heavy curtain, so you didn't see my feet sticking out underneath, and I could see how you opened my old art portfolios and brought out yellowing sketches, half-erased studies of figures, blurred drafts of compositions made almost invisible by the dust and the passage of the years. You examined my personal objects, letters bearing my name, on the desk, books with my initials, and when you rummaged through some volumes, you discovered the diary of my father, the general, arranged by me as I extracted the paragraphs relating to his personal, not military, life from the reports sent to the staff from the colonies, which the authorities handed over to me and which I never showed my mother. Did you read it all? You stayed quite a while leafing through it, and you often stopped to read whole pages, so that, although you may not have read it completely, you inevitably must have found out about the story of the two women, because, however few pages you may have read, in all of them, no matter what the general was speaking of, there was a reference to them. Did you read the story of the paintings? Surely you did. It is told in the last pages of the notebook; and from behind the curtain, I saw how you dwelled on those pages particularly.

As usual, upon entering the rooms of the elderly woman, you found her next to the window, sitting upright, dressed in blue and gray silk; the wind was moving the long, white, embroidered curtains rhythmically, and only the noise of the willow's foliage, stirred by the breeze, and the song of the birds in the garden altered the silence around her. She turned her nacreous face to you, with her dark glasses and her cordial smile. And you, Alice, that afternoon, now knew the truth about all the faces populating that room: Rudolph was not a scientist, and he lived in a far wing of the house; the strategist-general did not die under normal circumstances, nor was his life an uninterrupted string of success, happiness, and well-being capriciously cut short by sudden madness, as the old woman told you; the women who contemplated each other from their respective canvases had not died because, you told yourself, she at least was one of them, and although the other's face reminded you of someone, your suspicion was satisfied with the information you had uncovered, and, momentarily convinced, you forgot about the footsteps that, as you climbed the stairs, you would hear coming from the invalid's room and other details, such as the elderly woman's constant gesture of pushing back her dark glasses, as if she were afraid that someone would snatch them from her face or simply that they would slip from her nose, fall to the floor, and leave her eyes exposed. You also forgot about her original order to cover the mirrors with black veils.

They died, she repeated when you asked her again about the two women in the paintings, and now, with knowledge of the truth, you were surprised that so distinguished a lady would tell such a lie. However, Alice, that assertion, uttered as she turned her dark glasses toward the black veils that covered the mirrors, was not a lie, and like the strategist-general about whom the elderly woman would murmur *he never understood,* you did not understand either, although you started from the same data as the general (the rendezvous of the two women, their gazes, the paintings — in short, everything you read in the strategist's manuscripts). You had at your disposal more means than he to solve the mystery that caused his suffering, madness, and death: the visits to the other old woman and the readings.

Did the hands of the other elderly woman also shake as they removed the objects given by my mother the day before? Did she also ceaselessly fondle them, with that half-avid, half-satisfied smile on her lips, as you were reading? Were you amused by the similarity between the two, in their daily gifts to you of rings, bracelets, laces, handkerchiefs, and how one took from you what the other had given? Did you ask a servant or member of the other household whether, after you left, during the night they heard the laments, moans, and weeping of their mistress, as I heard those of my elderly mother, lying on the bed and clutching to her breast the objects she had removed from you, kissing them with a mixture of adoration and frenzy, alone in her room and without her dark glasses? If the curiosity that drove you to enter my room had induced you to climb the stairs very slowly, making no noise so as not to warn the elderly woman of your arrival, and you had spied through the keyhole of the door to her room, as I did, you would have seen the false semi-invalid and sightless woman drag from under the bed a trunk from which she pulled out dresses, handkerchiefs, articles of clothing, and adornment that she wore long ago to her rendezvous with the other woman and pick out those she was going to give you, then hide the trunk again, put on her dark glasses, and sit down, motionless, by the window in order to receive you, adorn you with the chosen articles, and keep those you were wearing—the ones that, the day before, another elderly woman had given you—which later she would kiss passionately, a thousand and one times, all night long. Overcome with weeping and nostalgia, she would crush them ardently, desperately, in an attempt to possess the one who formerly wore them; she would kiss them and run them over her entire body, within the four walls of that old woman's room, dominated by the portraits of two young, beautiful women who, as they contemplated each other, possessed each other forever.

But not even if you had witnessed the scene I have just described to you, which is only to explain—for you—the noise of footsteps coming from the elderly woman's room that you would hear as you went up, not even then, Alice, would you have managed to discover the reason for her isolation, the pretend blindness, and the exchange of articles and objects that the two elderly women accomplished through your person. After the general's death and after reading about his tortured experiences and feelings (could they possibly have been the product of his sickly imagination?), I followed my mother on her last appearance into the outside world. She attended the opera alone, attired in a white dress, and occupied a box opposite that of another woman, also dressed in white. For the entire performance, they stared at each other through their respective opera glasses. The scene, identical to the one recounted by the general in his writings, offered only one difference: when the music ended, as they stopped staring at each other and took the opera glasses away from their faces, both, at the same time, dried a tear. And they never again met.

The general's wife, my mother, stayed in bed for a long time, because of a sickness the doctors diagnosed as a nervous disorder. That was when I discovered the first wrinkles in her face. After that, she did not leave the house again. I attended the opera several times with the intention of seeing the other woman, but she never again went to the theater or the parks or places in the city where, according to the general's account, she would appear to meet my mother. And, as if by mutual agreement, they stopped seeing each other.

Neither I, Alice, like the general who *never understood,* as the elderly woman tells you, nor you, would have managed to understand or—to put it more fairly—even guess at the unusual behavior of these two women who lived many years adoring each other, always in search of each other, but who met only to contemplate one other (the sole expression of their love), and who suddenly stopped seeing each other, if it had not been for you, Alice, for the deductions drawn from your readings, selected by my elderly mother, to which I listened from behind the door: *He who possesses the gift of beauty dies young, if he wishes to die beautiful. Others will possess that beauty in him, but he will struggle in a world of inferior forms, possessing only himself or, even worse, his equal, should he find him in his path. Then both suffer a sad fate, that of never separating, for after the exultant period of elation, when the beauty of one is reflected in the beauty of the other—reciprocal mirrors of charm and grace—then this very indissolubility condemns them eventually to reproach each other for the deterioration wrought in them by the years—sickness, old age, and death—simply because they display themselves to each other, or, what amounts to the same thing, contemplate each other. Only equals who cease to exist for the world of corruptible forms at the moment when they enjoy full possession of their beauty, before the onset of decrepitude has damaged them, will remain eternally beautiful in the immutable mirror that each has been for the other.*

As you read, Alice, you raised your eyes toward the elderly woman's dark glasses, and immediately afterwards, you stared at the portraits of the two women who, as they contemplate each other, possess each other triumphantly, forever—was that gesture accidental, although a revelation to me? Or how many times did she make you read that passage from a romantic novel, in which one of the characters, after death has snatched away his beloved from his very arms, wanted to blind himself so that the image of his beloved would be the last thing he would see and his eyes retain?

Now do you understand, Alice?

ONCE UPON A TIME*

Once upon a Time's blond curls grew back, *One Left to Tell It* mentally wrote under the linden trees as he looked at the white form of his sister, standing with her back to him on the other side of the lake. After inhaling the smell of the bushes and <u>reminding himself not to forget</u> — when he evoked that moment at a later time — to join the impression of that fragrance to the uniform matte blue of the midafternoon sky and to the pleasant breeze that cooled the garden after five o'clock, he turned his feverish attention again to *Once upon a Time,* whose curls had indeed grown back.

The knowledge of this objective fact, recently acquired by *One Left to Tell It*'s mind, was followed by the presentiment of sudden changes that could affect the surrounding calm already fixed and described in his memory for a future story: the midafternoon light faded the red, blue, and violet of the flowers in the park, dulled the green of the leaves and trees, and threw shadows on the pink facade of the house and on the dusty gravel in the garden. If silence were a boat, you could say the world was riding in it at that very moment, and . . . *One Left to Tell It* stopped thinking about silence: it was broken by the flapping wings of a bird that startled him, took flight nearby, and reinstated him to an even greater degree in the reality from which he was condemned never to leave. *Once upon a Time* was going to cause serious problems because of her hair. He guessed it just by seeing her with her back to him, still reflected in the lake (he said to

*This story contains references to two Spanish children's songs:

I am Count Laurel's young widow / I want to marry someone / but I don't know who he could be.

Let it rain, let it rain / O Virgin of the Cave / The little birds are singing / the clouds are getting thicker / Yes, yes! No, no! / Let the rain pour down! / And shatter the windowpanes in the train station!

himself that, when he remembered it, he mustn't forget that the waters of the lake barely rippled as they distorted his sister's white dress reflected over the wild water lilies and blurred it into a diluted, slippery veil that covered them).

No, he couldn't see *Once upon a Time*'s face or, consequently, her expression; but because she kept running her hand over the curls on the back of her neck and tugging at the ends of her locks with quick, nervous jerks, *One Left to Tell It* understood: his sister was about to have hysterics.

If he so wished, he could recite everything that would happen to, in, and with *Once upon a Time* before it happened. Indeed, he could move the account of the events forward to the crisis, because the events destined to shape them imminently had already happened on more than one occasion, and he had recorded their details in his memory in order to remember and tell them when necessary. Such a task was expected of him, such a duty was demanded of him, that's what he was. Nothing, no one was preventing him from starting to tell . . . No, no, he repeated to himself in an effort to overcome the temptation. Nothing, no one was preventing him; but was anyone asking him? No, no one. Besides, he said to himself, if, instead of being on the alert now for everything that might happen, so he could remember and tell it in due time, he concentrated on remembering and telling what had already happened (even though it might be the same thing), then, when the unpredictable moment finally arrived for him to tell whatever had just happened, how in the world could he remember and tell that what had happened was that he remembered and told that he was remembering what was happening, because he remembered that it had already happened? No, it was impossible. If he began now to remember and tell what had already happened, it would be impossible for him to pay attention to everything happening at that moment, in order to record it in his memory and be able to remember and tell it later. No, his was not an easy, tranquil existence, he sighed under the linden trees, the best location from which to command the widest possible panorama of the garden—only he and *Once upon a Time* were in it now, he confirmed—and at the same time to see the only entrance with access to the park (the garden gate) and the main door to the house; mandatory observation points by which he meticulously apprised himself of the entrances and exits, comings and goings of the residents there, signs of activities—even the most insignificant ones—that could not be overlooked lest he lose the thread of the events, of their complete development, of their implications and outcomes, should there be any, because one day (and his whole life, effort, and existence pointed toward that day) he would account for them. No, his was not a tranquil existence. How long could that existence endure the never-ending task of patiently tracking, step by step, the lives of everyone around it—he, a person with no curiosity about what didn't concern him? How long could he endure, compelled to take note of sorrows and happiness, adventures and failures experienced by the others and unintelligible to him because, condemned forever to be an observer and listener, he had never felt what he heard and observed? Hearing and observation alternated with a dizzying rapidity that allowed him meager respite to meditate on them and understand them. And his memory? What if that unspecified day for telling everything he had seen and heard took so long to arrive that the dreaded phenomenon should take place, that his memory, already crammed full of recollections, would have room for no more? His memory weighed him down; it was a gravestone covering that vast precinct where all his recollections lived, on whose marble he alone carved and read the inscriptions about the lives of the residents in the pink house so as not to condemn them to the silence, oblivion, and darkness of a tomb in danger of being sealed up by that gravestone—his memory—if no one held it up or no one remembered it. How long must he bear that burden of memories? How long must he periodically review them to make sure he hadn't misplaced a single one? How long must he arrange them, number them, group them according to type, color, similarity, or relationship, and at the same time record them in the general chronology? When will the day come, he would often sigh, when everyone around him disappears and only one—he—will be left to tell it? One left to tell it. Why not be the one in the telling? Why not be a blue blood, a blue-blooded prince, blond and brave, with silver chain mail, a diamond sword, and armies of fiery dragons to kill; blue-blooded, with an enchanted castle, snowy clouds, and swirling dust raised by war; blue-blooded, with tongue-tied fairy godmothers who want to bestow happiness and instead turn souls to stone; blue-blooded, a wound on his forehead, awakening outside the forest. . . ? Why not a fearsome pirate with seas of rum and a peg leg, the scourge of ports and taverns, and an inscription on his hook? Why not rain or wind or algae that are born and die? Or a giant from the forces of evil with hellish eyes, tongues of ice, and skin made of a thousand barbs, slain when one hundred knights chop off its head with scarlet daggers? And only one was left to tell it. Always? He was left. Left. Not the others? To whom does the one who is left tell it, if only one—he—is left? No, no, he said to himself, it is forbidden to think, it is forbidden to waste time by indulging in vague thoughts—neither his time nor his attention, now fixed again on *Once upon a Time*, who was about to stop examining the length of her curls and shudder with a bloodcurdling scream. She will hug herself hard—guessed *One Left to Tell It*—as if she were clinging to some imaginary loved one; without letting go of herself, she will writhe, shaken by a deep, indefinite pain; her straw hat will fall into the lake or at her feet, and she might trample it.

Once upon a Time's pale blue eyes were hollow, absent, and empty; they traveled over the magnolias, the oleanders. She progressed along the avenue of banana trees with slow, sinuous steps. Now, was she crying as she ran toward the maze formed of dwarf pines? *One Left to Tell It*, a short distance away, was about to reach her; he couldn't see her cheeks, dry or wet, but he heard a weak moan when his sister stopped, trembling, before the maze's entrance from whose green archway hung the warning "No Admittance. Someone Is Getting Lost Inside"; she dropped to the grass, staining her white organdy dress, and murmured, "*Once upon a Time?* Who? Me? Where? When is 'Once upon'? Is 'Once upon' only once?" With a questioning look, she asked the sun-dappled earth of midafternoon and the August light of a sky already waiting for night to fall over the pink house, far from the trees. Quick movements of her head traced a circular sweep of the surroundings at which *Once upon a Time*'s pale, disfigured face gazed and from which her vacant stare and surprised smile separated her. "And 'before'?" Tears fell on the ants pulled from the grass by her twitching fingers. "Was 'before' 'once upon another time'? Was I, *Once upon a Time,* in that 'once upon another time'? And 'once upon other times,' many 'once upon other times' that aren't one time — where, when are they? Where, when are those many 'once upon other times'? How many are many 'once upon other times'?" The bewildered, weak voice became a scream, and she shrieked with her face hidden in her hands. "But . . . 'once upon a time' isn't 'once upon another time'!" And she reaffirmed "No, it isn't," in a barely audible tone, which rose again, "Can 'once upon a time' which isn't 'once upon another time' be in 'another time' although it may not be 'once upon another time'? No, if 'once upon a time' isn't 'once upon another time,' it can't be in 'another time' either," she whispered slowly, her unmoving eyes staring at the trunk of a tree; and she broke off her gaze and her brief silence, beat the ground with her fists, and screamed, "Can *Once upon a Time* only be once? And be only in 'one time'?"

Crying, she hugged *One Left to Tell It,* who was upset because it was impossible to comfort his sister and answer her questions, since thinking about them and answering them would prevent him from listening to *Once upon a Time*'s words and observing her gestures and expressions in order to record them in his memory. He stroked her hair while her voice, intensified by anguish or fear, implored, "Is once long? Is it short? When once is over, where does it go?" Her nails dug into *One Left to Tell It*'s shoulders; he quickly noted her string of questions in his mind, anxious to utter some word effectively, to take even one second from the time needed to clock his sister's broken sobs, check how violently her breast was heaving, observe how she clawed at her face, and hear once again, "Is once brief or is it short? Is once now? Am I, *Once upon a Time,* now?" Convulsed with a shudder, eyes wide open, she violently seized her brother's arms, shaking him. "Is now short? Is now long?"

Tears ran down *One Left to Tell It*'s cheeks, which were flushed with helplessness; then he was bewildered by his sister's unexpected, bright singsong: "Now is once! Now I am *Once upon a Time* once! Here I am in 'once'! Here, here I am in 'now'!" She took him by both hands and made him dance with her to the rhythm of her song, "Now I am once. Now I am once. Now I am once . . ." And they continued whirling on the grass; her face was flushed, her blue eyes sparkled, and her lips parted in loud peals of laughter: "It's raining 'is.' It's raining 'time'! It's raining 'now'!" Until the song suddenly went silent, the dance stopped, and, motionless, she whispered, "And later? After 'now' is it another 'now' or a 'later'?" She threw herself to her knees on the ground again and, pummeling her head, exclaimed, "'Once' is now! What is 'once' in another 'now'? What is 'once' in 'later'? Where is it? What is, where is *Once upon a Time* later?" Bent double, she moaned the reply, "'Once upon Another Time,' that's what I would be! — But 'Once upon Another Time' is someone else, not me! Is this tree trunk a different trunk later?" she burst out in a faltering voice. "That wallflower! Will it be this one or a different one after 'now'?" she shouted, almost losing her voice, at a clump of wallflowers. "Will that red be a different red when 'now' ends?" she exclaimed, looking at the geraniums. "No, they won't be different, because since I can only *be* once, I will always see that red! But my curls are short over and over and long over and over! They are 'over and over,'" she repeated, her voice increasingly choked. "But I — 'once,' only 'once'! Short? Long? And later? *Once upon a Time* can't be later."

One Left to Tell It started to tremble. There was panic in his sister's eyes. Yes, he thought, only panic enlarges the pupil so much; only panic can make her behave so erratically. "Will there be a 'once upon another time' where *Once upon a Time* can be when she finishes her own 'once,' or will that other 'once' belong to another *Upon a Time* that takes place inside her?" she whispered, her frightened voice already exhausted.

"In the depths of silence a fire is raging," he said to himself, or the phrase said it to itself in *One Left to Tell It*'s mind. How did that phrase manage suddenly to escape from one of the many trunks of phrases carefully locked up in the hold of the drunken boat, his memory? "In the depths of silence a fire is raging," the phrase repeated itself, to its great delight, he thought, furious and bewildered as always when a phrase, a memory, or a picture escaped from the archives of the past and had a fine time turning up in his mind and inserting itself among those pictures or sentences of the present that had been recently taken from reality. "In the depths of silence a fire is raging," he listened again, while he frantically pummeled his head to silence it and take the opportunity offered by *Once upon a Time*'s brief silence to address a few comforting words to her.

"In the depths of silence a fire is raging." No, it had nothing to do with one of those phrases that rebelled against remaining still forever in the past, from the moment in which they were uttered, one of those phrases that was overcome by a madness for freedom and tried to emerge from *One Left to Tell It*'s oceanic memory, reach the surface, and fly up to a thermal current that would never carry them again. No, it was not a question of one of those incorrigible phrases that felt the need to repeat themselves to themselves now and again in order to go on believing in their own existence, those escapees from memory that required so much time and effort to return to the mouth of the person who uttered them, to the correct setting and moment in the past. "In the depths of silence a fire is raging": the voice from beyond the grave was now heard behind *One Left to Tell It*, who was now free from any doubt whether the phrase originated in his own mind or not, because *Once upon a Time* also heard it, or at least her brother assumed so when he saw her turn her disturbed gaze toward the place from which it was coming.

"In the depths of silence a fire is raging," hoarsely murmured Count Laurel, addressing his brother and sister. How could *One Left to Tell It* have doubted that it was a current phrase, since he was accustomed to hearing it almost daily from the mouth of Count Laurel, who would utter it during his solitary, late afternoon strolls along the shadiest, leafiest paths in the park to prevent the intense sunlight from striking his nonexistent person? How could he have confused the motto and basis for meditation of one of his brothers with a phrase from some other time? He pounded his head again angrily, this time in punishment for his unpardonable confusion. And he kept on pounding it, now with greater force and resentment against his mental mechanism because, overwhelmed with confusion and contradictions, he barely heard the beginning of the conversation between his brother and sister.

"The silence, the depths of silence and the raging fire—can they take place at the same time? Can they be over and over, like my hair which sometimes is long and at other times short, or like the night, which every twelve hours is in a 'once' that is different each time? Or can the silence, the depths of silence and the raging fire, be only 'once,' like me?" asked *Once upon a Time*, her reddened eyes staring at Count Laurel, who was muffled in his black cape and bent slightly over the white horse from which he had dismounted.

"'Once'? Be 'once' or over and over?" Instead of coming from a human throat, his voice seemed to emerge from within the ferrous breastplate glimpsed when the wind billowed his cape open like wings. "Be 'once'? Be over and over?" he repeated slowly, meditatively, as he absentmindedly fondled the hilt of his sword. "What odd questions you ask!" he thundered suddenly. "What do I know about being! What do I know about being and about hours and time! Problems of the living! As if you didn't know that I am dead! How many times must I repeat it to you to make you understand? Or could you be making fun of me, teasing me?"

The stertorous cries seemed to rumble and emerge from the bowels of the earth, from the tree trunks, from the caves of the now overcast evening sky; they seemed to have been generated by huge red boulders crashing against each other as they rolled down from the top of the highest mountains in the world toward the grounds of the house, which was on the point of quaking. As Count Laurel brandished his sword, he split the air with it; his horse ran away, but the cavernous exclamations must have frozen the animal's blood, because it stood still and motionless in the distance, its mane blowing in the wind.

"I'm dead! Dead! Do you understand?" He fixed empty purplish eye sockets on *Once upon a Time* and with a gaping, hollow smile, took one of her hands in his hard and frozen one. This contact, which to her felt like the swift, cold blade of a sharp hatchet, numbed the feeling in her hand. As a result, she screamed, not frightened by the proximity of the tenuous, wrinkled, ashen hide stuck to the bones of his face—a now familiar sight—but convinced that the Count had cut off her hand.

One Left to Tell It opened his mouth, ready to interfere, calm his brother's wrath, and soothe *Once upon a Time,* but he closed it again when the Count interrupted him: "And you, who are supposed to be gifted with the faculty for telling things well, let's see if you can explain and make her understand, once and for all, that I am dead. Dead! For ever and ever!"

One Left to Tell It agreed to his brother's request; just as he was about to carry it out, he held back to observe the change of mood that had come over the Count, who was stooped over, with his shadow-arms hanging by his sides: after sighing so deeply that the protective armor over his hollow chest creaked, his scarlet, lipless mouth emitted a noise like sea waves receding after breaking against the rocks, and he calmed down. Very slowly, he drew on his black velvet gloves and stretched out a hand to *Once upon a Time* to help her rise up from the grass where she still remained, confused and silent. Now that the Count had vented his anger, the horse returned to its master, who stroked its mane as he whispered, "Dead. Forever." From the dark, empty eye sockets flowed tears that were alternately red, violet, green, or gold; *One Left to Tell It* decided that such a variety of colors was probably due to the changes and variations of the late afternoon light in the garden as it fell on the flowers and trees and was reflected in the Count's tears. Although tears usually followed the Count's outburst of uncontrollable anger when any of the other residents of the house was responsible for an unimportant incident or innocent remark that unwittingly recalled and corroborated his deceased status to him, *One Left to Tell It* said to himself that he had not seen Count Laurel cry so hard for some time. His stylized black shape was bent over his horse; he hugged it and whispered once again, "Dead. Forever."

Once upon a Time didn't understand the meaning of forever, but she suppressed the question intended to ascertain whether he was dead forever in 'once' or in 'another time' so that she could listen to the words uttered by her brother, sitting dispiritedly on his horse, his scarlet mouth pressed to the animal's coat. The Count's position saddened *One Left to Tell It,* but it also made it more difficult for him to perform his duty, to interpret the account fashioned by that hoarse, impersonal voice, a monotonous rumble with no intensity or nuances, the compendium of the echo of his own echo ceaselessly resounding inside a distant hollow enclosure, where it had been shut up for centuries and from which it now emerged to fling badly modulated words over a horse's coat. "Dead. Forever. In the depths of silence a fire is raging. That is where the hanged man's tree grows. Was I hanged? Executed? Killed in the war? No one knows what or who sent me to the depths of silence—whether an undated arrow or a silver dagger engraved with a maxim about love, a well-aimed sword on the battlefield or a daring adventure with an impossible return . . . No, no one can learn what caused my death, because I wasn't killed, nor did I die. Quite simply, I was born already dead. Her mouth named me as already dead. Her voice sings that she is Count Laurel's widow, and she was born as my widow. Only a name. She sings nothing else about me, adds nothing to my deceased status, not ancestry or deeds, youth or defeats, thoughts or history. Only a name without a past; dead; and even so, I exist only if she pronounces it."

Who had existed under that name? Who was he, and what had he been like? Why didn't she sing it in her song? If she was his widow, she had married him and had known him before. She knew who he was, what he had been like. He would order her to tell him when he met her. But what fleeting encounters! He was shot from a mouth into the rushing wind that quickly carried the words of the song far, far away, bullets of sound fired by the lips of the person who claimed to be his widow. After the repercussive burst of utterance, the words rose through the air until they disintegrated, and he, one of those words, remained for scarcely a fraction of a second on the young widow's lips, with barely enough time to make his request. Whenever someone (a girl, a young lady, or an old woman) began the song that mentioned him, he would resolve to cling to the lips about to pronounce his name; unyielding, he would stop inside the mouth; he would unsheathe his sword and thrust it into the palate to paralyze movement and prevent his expulsion into the outside world as only a name and deceased. But the voice would emerge from the singer's throat stronger than his sword and with such speed that as soon as he was named, he would lose his sense of direction across the space through which he was tumbling, turning somersaults until he was dizzy, far, far away from the young widow who went on with her song, searching for romance and depriving him of the only balm that could soothe his anguish: to make some allusion, however slight, to the person his name concealed in some unknown time and place.

"Only a name. And deceased," whispered the Count, hugging his horse before *Once upon a Time*'s uncomprehending but affectionate gaze. "A name she reveals to no one. No man exists behind my name. No story. Just silence. And the icy winds of my own ignorance that lash me pitilessly. Only silence and anguish, ravenous serpents sucking up my nothingness, wounding it with a thousand fiery tongues until they poison it with the venom of 'Perhaps he did exist, but someone has forgotten to tell it.' There is no one behind my name. Only silence and death, snow burning in the depths of its raging fire, because death is alive, and there is no place for names in its palace of crucified doves. It doesn't accept names, or silence, or waiting, but hunts them down with its bitches: shadows, loneliness, and emptiness. And fear." Would he soon drown in the great lake of nothingness? Would the needles of its treacherous water pierce him when his name ceased to exist? If the young widow should acquire a new husband, she would stop being Count Laurel's widow and singing about him. Then who would name him? If no one utters a name, where does it end up?

"Don't worry," *Once upon a Time* tried to comfort him. "As long as she wants to get married and doesn't know who he could be, she will go on being your widow."

Alarmed, *One Left to Tell It* tried to advise his brother and sister not to mention that name: if *Who He Could Be* heard them, he might think he was being called and join them, then and there. In view of the Count's desolate appearance and *Once upon a Time*'s vacant expression, he thought, no presence could be as counterproductive now as *Who He Could Be,* always teetering erratically between a pained sigh and an endless moan. But aware of approaching footsteps, he said nothing.

The Happy Man emerged from the maze of dwarf pines, their greenness dulled by the late afternoon shadows; it seemed as if the growing semidarkness was turning them into stone homunculi. *The Happy Man* took down the sign hanging from the arch that surmounted the entrance to the maze; on it was the warning "No Admittance. Someone Is Getting Lost Inside." He exclaimed, while continuing to hop, jump, and do arm and leg exercises, "It's not possible! I don't understand it! I have spent two days and two nights inside the maze trying to lose myself, and I swear I still haven't succeeded."

Sneezing and shivering, he stammered complaints: not only was he condemned to spend his life going everywhere without a shirt—his skin burning in the summer sun, freezing in the winter snows, softening in the rain, and getting goose pimples from the wind all year round—but in addition he was allowed to have nothing. Absolutely nothing! And sometimes, when he caught himself thinking, when he discovered that he had thoughts, memories, feelings, "I am aware that I exist; I, who may possess nothing, have an awareness of myself," he explained to his brothers and sister, and he ran toward the maze in a desperate attempt to lose himself.

It was already dark, and after taking the shivering, sweaty *Happy Man*'s pulse, Count Laurel advised him to go into the house and have something hot to drink, and then whispered into *One Left to Tell It*'s ear: "He has a high fever. This pneumonia was predictable: always shirtless." The whispering annoyed his interlocutor, who was obliged to listen both to the Count and to *The Happy Man*—panting but still skipping—ask his brothers and sister, "Although I do waste energy with these stupid, boring exercises, it is also true that at the same time I am getting healthier. What do you think? Do you lose more by wasting energy and having your health, or is it better—if not to lose, at least not to acquire anything—to give up having your health and not lose energy?"

The two brothers and the sister looked at each other, surprised and dubious at first, then thoughtful and speculative. That is, not all three: *One Left to Tell It* avoided all surprise, thought, and speculation about the problem posed by *The Happy Man* so he could devote himself to observing the surprise, doubts, thoughts, and speculations of the others.

They chose not to enter the first sitting room in the house open to the hall; they passed by its door on tiptoe, trying not to make any noise. The *Virgin of the Cave* lived there, and by mutual agreement, the residents avoided her and her complaints. "Where, where do they expect me to get all that rain? Help me, help me collect some rain!" They half-opened the door to the second room: in the semidarkness, they could see Sleeping Beauty, stretched out on a green velvet sofa. They shut her in again. *The Happy Man* and *One Left to Tell It* were dreadfully anxious; they paled merely thinking that they might have wakened her, remembering one occasion when Sleeping Beauty woke up and they discovered that when awake, she was not only extremely homely but malicious. She drank coffee nonstop to avoid drowsiness, and to show them that she knew how to spin perfectly well without pricking herself ("That's slander! That's gossip, and I know who said it," she would say, turning her crossed eyes toward the next room where one of the witches of the house lived), she was determined to sew a shirt for *The Happy Man,* while she insisted on telling *One Left to Tell It* all the dreams played out in her mind during the centuries spent in sleep.

Noisy shouts came from behind the third door; they recognized the voices of Snow White and the dwarfs. *One Left to Tell It* did his duty and looked through the keyhole to take note of whatever was happening: that morning, Snow White had insisted again on sunbathing in the park, and while five little dwarfs were doing their best to disguise her suntan by applying flour to her skin, Grumpy, red with fury, was scolding the lot of them: "More flour! More flour! Her skin must look as white as snow! She's naturally dark, so who gets the bright idea of taking a sunbath? She looks like a gypsy! Idiot! Do you think it's so easy to find a near-sighted prince to kiss you and wake you every time someone gets the notion to tell your ridiculous story?"

One Left to Tell It saw only six dwarfs. They found the seventh, Dopey, trembling in a corner of the next room; he was huddled in the draperies and weeping copiously. Unable to endure the arguments between Snow White and the other dwarfs, he would flee at the first signs of an outburst. He was afraid that one day, as a result of those quarrels—the cause of demonstrations in favor of Snow White by some of the dwarfs and in favor of Grumpy by the others—they would not make up as they usually did: they would decide to separate forever, and he would be left alone in the world. Whimpering, he explained this in sign language to *One Left to Tell It* as soon as he saw him enter the room in the company of Count Laurel, *Once upon a Time,* and

The Happy Man. One Left to Tell It, with the tearful Dopey clinging to him, tried to explain how absurd his fears were, because even if the dwarfs and Snow White should have a quarrel and decide to follow their destinies separately, there would always be people in the world to tell the story of the seven dwarfs and the white maiden, and when they did, it would reunite them again in a common destiny. But he said nothing. *The Happy Man* was uttering cries of alarm, "No, no, don't cover my chest! Don't cover me or I will be consumed with unhappiness!"

Moved by Dopey's tears, *The Happy Man* had stroked his round head affectionately, and in order to show appreciation for the tender gesture from that trembling, feverish hand, the little dwarf had tried to wrap *The Happy Man* in a blanket when he heard him sneeze. *The Happy Man*'s panic at what was intended for well-meaning affection convinced the dwarf of his own uselessness and plunged him into greater unhappiness, at least that was *One Left to Tell It*'s interpretation of Dopey's expression when he raised his tiny hands to his enormous pink head and pulled on his Dumbo-like ears. *Once upon a Time* took him on her lap, and everyone accepted Count Laurel's suggestion, which was especially meant for *The Happy Man,* shivering and strangely restless: drink a cup of hot tea. "One cup or several," repeated the Count, since there were many cups ready for teatime, and only then did *One Left to Tell It* notice where they were.

Even as he entered the house, he thought he saw Alice disappearing beyond the garden gate and the White Rabbit running through the evening shadows as he took his watch from his waistcoat pocket and exclaimed: "Oh Lord! I shall be late! This time I intend to tell the Duchess I don't feel like looking for her gloves or her fan. That's that!" Later, because his attention was absorbed by Dopey's fearful presentiments, when he entered the sitting room where they now were, *One Left to Tell It* didn't see the large table in front of the tree where the March Hare, the Mad Hatter, and the Dormouse usually had tea. He smiled as he saw the night behind the windowpanes and thought that it would be six o'clock in the room if the Mad Hatter had been there—

having quarreled with Time, he always lived in six o'clock; that's why his tea was endlessly ready for . . . "Who could have forgotten to have his tea?" said *Once upon a Time.* "Making me leave home just to order heads cut off!" They recognized the Queen of Hearts's voice grumbling along the hall. Someone, somewhere, had started to tell or to read Alice's adventures, and interrupting their tea, the March Hare, the Mad Hatter, and the Dormouse had disappeared to go to the narrator's mouth.

Shaking with a chill, *The Happy Man*'s hand almost let go of the cup. "Happy . . . happy . . . But I always have that damned cold, I always have a headache, a fever." In fact, his bleary eyes, his hoarse voice, the wet handkerchief bound around his forehead to relieve his headache, his irritated nose, his dull expression didn't correspond with the picture of happiness. His lips, disfigured by endless chapping and blisters, persistently holding an expression meant to portray the radiant smile of a happy man—did they not depict a grimace of profound misery? "Happy, happy . . . ," he went on whispering, while with gloved hand, Count Laurel made him drink more hot tea. "Always hounded by that witch's threat," he shouted, raising his eyes to the ceiling, toward the floor above, where one of the witches lived; she amused herself by threatening to change him into the richest man in the world if he didn't take her for his wife.

"I'm not allowed. I couldn't marry her even if I loved her!" he said, his elbows resting on the table, head in his hands. "Since I can't possess anything, I can't even have a family!"

"For the time being you're happy, aren't you?" *Once upon a Time* began to comfort him. "You have always been poor, you have never possessed anything, right?" But after a few seconds of silence, she continued anxiously, "Are you happy once, or over and over? Are you a man and are you happy at the same time, in a single 'once'? Do you continue being happy and a man when 'once' ends? Is 'once' brief or short? Tell me, I need to know, because I only am 'once'! What will I be when 'once' ends?"

Once upon a Time's crying and the crash of her cup on the floor woke Dopey, who was asleep in her lap; he bumped his huge head against the pastry-laden table and attempted to ask whether they knew of any dwarf who had ever been cured of his muteness and how it had happened; but since he was mute, he was unable to formulate any question.

Soaked with sweat and shivering, but unexpectedly bursting with joy, *The Happy Man* suddenly got up and, turning cartwheels around the table where his brothers and sister were sitting, exclaimed to *Once upon a Time,* "Why cry, eh? Why despair when you can count on the support and love of a brother like me, brimming with possessions and riches and eager to lose it all, even my shirt?"

And he took the girl with the vacant gaze in his arms and danced with her before the nervous, ill-humored *One Left to Tell It.* Count Laurel's words, whispered in his ear ("Our brother is delirious; the fever is making him believe what he most fears: that he is a rich man"), prevented him from hearing *The Happy Man*'s promises to his dance partner, "We will buy many, many 'over and overs'! All the 'over and overs' you want! All the 'over and overs' in the world and all the spare 'over and overs' of all the 'over and overs' in the world! All, all for you!"

"No, no," *Once upon a Time* interrupted his generous offer. "This isn't about buying many 'over and overs.' What I need are many 'once upons.' I can only be once, not over and over."

"No problem," laughed *The Happy Man,* almost whirling his sister in the air in a reckless waltz. "We'll buy 'once upon' after 'once upon'! Loads, heaps of 'once upons'! If you are in a 'once upon' and don't like it, you throw it away—it's as simple as that! You try another one! If you are in a 'once upon' and you feel happy in it, we will order millions of copies of it! It's up to you! We will buy many, loads, whole forests of 'once upons' of every size and color! 'Once upons' made of silk, of foam, of precious stones, of tulle, of light, of yellow beams."

Exhausted, he fell on the daisy-patterned carpet next to the tree whose foliage was stunted by the ceiling, and, unaware of *Once upon a Time*'s sudden disappearance, he went on with his wild plans, gasping, "Yes, yes! The best 'once upons' will be for you! Where do you suppose they sell them?" he wondered, rolling on the floor with closed eyes, hands clasped behind the back of his neck. "Time! We must ask him for an appointment immediately."

One Left to Tell It sighed, relieved by *Once upon a Time*'s disappearance: with her ceaseless questioning, her condition required the most attention. How long would she take to return? he wondered, sinking into an easy chair, prepared to take a little rest and enjoy his sister's absence. He hoped that whoever had taken her into his mouth and had begun a story with her, saying "Once upon a time," would have enough imagination to tell it at great length. And he hoped that the child who was supposed to fall asleep or to be amused by it would take a very, very long time. He dreaded her returns: weakly, *Once upon a Time* would tell what they had made her be. Sometimes the narrator would begin by saying "Once," and as she was preparing to be *Once upon a Time,* he would go on "there was," and then she had to go round and round herself so many times in order to turn into *There Was* that she became dizzy and could barely find out what she was to be next. But whatever they made her be, she always returned complaining, furious at *Happily Ever After:* if she liked the story into which they put her, he always reached the narrator's voice too soon; or if she didn't like it, he arrived too late. On one occasion, she came back ready to kill *Happily Ever After* because he ended a story just as they turned her into a toad. And a toad she remained until someone broke the spell when he continued the story.

Sunk into the armchair, *One Left to Tell It* watched how night darkened the windowpanes. Little by little, the residents of the house would leave. It was the best time for telling stories out there in the world, and when his brothers and sisters were away, he enjoyed the greatest peace. Soon the arguments would cease on the floor above, where Wendy was refusing to give the Lost Boys her care and affection, threatening to leave them if they didn't grow up once and for all. But even if someone got the idea to tell about their adventures in Never-Never Land and took them away, he would still not have an opportunity to rest: the Milkmaid would appear, complaining again about her spilled milk; the forces of evil would arrive, rebelling against their eternal fate of being vanquished and thrashed by the forces of good, arguing that they had not chosen to represent any moral category . . .

Absorbed in his thoughts, he noticed a new presence in the room. Why had he not seen *Who He Could Be* come in? His face, the color of purple glass, was surrounded by shadows; he moved toward the window; his condemned-man's eyelids closed over eyes that always reflected the sum total of what he was — expectation. "An insect has more life; smoke is less gray," he murmured, referring to himself. "A tear has greater weight; a memory, more presence."

"Only a name, and deceased," Count Laurel's black cape swayed gently beyond the darkness, which was accentuated by the sound of his raspy voice. "Neither a man nor a story exists behind my name," he continued in a dialogue between people doomed to row in the changeless current of stagnant waters, in a phrase from the song of a widow whom they would never know.

"But a name exists and suggests something. The flight of a butterfly from its larval state has more meaning than I." Fragile glass tinkled near the window. *Who He Could Be* stared into the night. "The dust that a dead, faded butterfly leaves on your fingers is more visible than I."

"A name with no man and no story is only silence. And in the depths of silence a fire is raging," the Count's voice came from a well where no one ever drowned.

"But you are a name, and you suffer. If people say it, a name can feel the lily's sweet lash deep within; if they forget it, it can feel the prickle of ivy slowly covering it; if they utter it, it can feel the wild, beating wings of the bird that loves the country and flies in springtime. No one calls me, utters me, or forgets me, because no one calls, utters, or forgets nothingness." And after a sigh that was visible in the room because the moonlight quivered in passing through it, *Who He Could Be* added, "Nobody can find me either."

"You aren't nothing," the Count tried to cheer him, united in the conspiratorial brotherhood of nobodies about whom they both knew. "You speak, you are."

"Because I am nothingness in waiting," answered *Who He Could Be,* in a voice that had escaped from nobody's dream. "What wouldn't I give for a name, a silence, and a raging fire even if I were dead—I, only some kind of relation to who knows what, an empty word used to replace someone, and I don't even know who he is."

"Perhaps you will find yourself at last," said the Count with a tight feeling in his throat and black tulips springing from his eyes, because if his widow fell in love with *Who He Could Be* and married him, she would cease singing that she was Count Laurel's widow, and then no one would utter his name.

"I am unfindable. You can find the person I am replacing and I don't know; I am not even his shadow or echo, but you can't find me." The yellowish mist of grief clouded the purple glass of his face.

"I am searching," said the Count.

"I am waiting," murmured *Who He Could Be.* "I am waiting," he repeated, and his note broke the blue but intense melancholy with which the symphony of silence was about to reverberate around the room until it was spoiled by the dull repetition. And above the table and the tarts and the cups of still-hot tea, the air in the room was weighed down by the abruptness of the echo that acknowledges in its own echo the final acceptance of condemnation to forever.

In the dark, the brief dialogue (or prayer? wondered *One Left to Tell It,* in order to file it, already properly classified, in his memory) between the Count's long black cape at the back of the room and, by the window, *Who He Could Be,* a tinkling, fragile piece of glass always on the verge of breaking, lulled *The Happy Man* into a fitful sleep and made *One Left to Tell It* drowsy; the silence startled him when the monotonous voices stopped. He discovered Dopey's absence and also the calm in the next room, which Snow White and the dwarfs had occupied earlier. The arguments between Wendy and the Lost Boys had ceased, as had the quarrels between the gnomes and the insolent fairies, the maddening creaking of the knife grinder to whom traitors flocked to sharpen the blades of their daggers, the exclamations of brave princes beseeching heaven to change their destinies (they loathed killing the hundred-headed monster who had done them no harm, blood made them nauseous, and blond princesses bored them to death). To judge from the peacefulness, the house was half-deserted, its residents gone. Where were they being told? He couldn't make up his mind whether to go out into the garden to clear his head in the cool night air or to try to rest for a brief space of time in one of the empty rooms. But as he went out into the hall, he heard groans of pain and heavy steps shaking the floors and walls. Someone was returning, displeased with the story into which he had been introduced, he thought. A wounded dragon was crawling toward him. While he extracted a sword from one of its paws and bandaged it, the monster complained alternately about the sting of the disinfectant and about the storyteller whom fate had chosen for it: the tale recounted was the usual one, but instead of being killed by the knight, the dragon was only wounded, an accident more painful than death, it affirmed; and this unfamiliar experience tinged with bewilderment the hundred red eyes on the monster's colossal mass of green-violet flesh.

No sooner had he taken care of the outraged dragon's paw and lain down on the sofa in the first room, where he had decided to shut himself off to rest, than a violent slam of the door and a woman's "I'm fed up! I can't take any more!" made him stand up in alarm. Facing him, the young widow was pulling black veils from her face, tearing her dismal skirts as she ran toward the curtains, drew them back, threw the French doors wide open, and cried, "Light! I want light and sun! Bright-colored dresses! Wide avenues to walk along, with rivers of people; ocean liners' decks where I can sit and take the sun next to a stranger who calls me by my Christian name, Juana, Margarita, even María, whatever it may be; restaurants with Gypsy music and the color of champagne, where the maître d' calls me madame or mademoiselle when I enter!"

And she wrapped herself in fabrics that were red and green, then blue, yellow, and scarlet, walking around the bedroom where neither light nor sun entered, but only the cold of night. "A passport that states 'unmarried' in gold letters; seas and continents of good-looking strangers with whom I could . . . talk, at least!" she shouted, throwing a flowerless vase against the mirror, which exploded into a thousand reflections of colored fabrics, black veils, and widow's faces reddened by convulsive sobs. These sobs were interrupted at intervals by rebellious declarations: "A widow? Never again! Never again! I won't be one! I won't!"

Over her torn dress, she put on a dressing gown the color of the seas she had wanted to cross and would never behold, and sitting on her bed, she fixed her staring green eyes on the distance beyond the half-open window and the curtains blowing in the wind, beyond the night and the garden. As she dried her tears, she gently touched the delicate skin of her cheeks and around her lips and eyes, looking for the wrinkles that *One Left to Tell It* was about to say were "Nonexistent, since you are in the prime of youth," but she was evidently well aware of this, because she exclaimed, "Why am I a widow so young? Why a widow without first having had marriage, love, and passion?" As soon as she was outside those four walls, she would fall madly in love with anyone she met in passing, were he the most repugnant evil goblin invented by the twisted human mind or the knight who was the most valiant but as cold and heavy as the sword brandished to mete out justice. But who would notice her? Who would guess how young and beautiful she was, if the entire world assumed, believed, that she looked grotesque or was dreadfully wicked because she was forced to repeat so often that she wanted to get married and didn't know who he could be? Her green eyes shone at maximum intensity, and she threw another flowerless vase against another mirror. "With all my strength, I could strangle the people who sing me!" she shouted, crushing a handkerchief in her fingers.

If she didn't calm down, thought *One Left to Tell It*, the young widow would finish off all the vases, mirrors, and handkerchiefs in the bedroom, as she did one night when she returned home in a rage after having been sung in a cabaret by an erotic-burlesque music hall singer, who confessed from the stage, "I can't find anyone," at which point a lasciviously bald man in his seventies responded, "Me, Me," and under an obscene mustache, his wine-stained mouth reviled her with, "I'm not getting married, but if you need a favor. . . ," causing a general laughter that still mortified her in her nightmares.

"Why am I a widow?" she repeated. "Why not Count Laurel's wife, since fate links me to this name? Why not meet *Who He Could Be*? And why not both at the same time: a countess and *Who He Could Be*'s lover? I am fed up, fed up with this centuries-long widowhood! With this empty bed—"

Someone knocked softly, and as she listened to the promising flattery coming from the other side of the door, the young widow renounced her fury and crying for a smile, hurriedly dried her tears, and arranged her red hair before the only un-damaged mirror in the bedroom. *One Left to Tell It* guessed that, when someone returned after having been told, he had found one of the young widow's many invitations, deposited daily in the rooms of every resident in the house, and *One Left to Tell It* decided to retire prudently through the half-open bal-cony window instead of confirming the identity of the night-strolling lover, for he could do it from the garden.

Now dawn was painting rosy borders on the sky. As he left the young widow's bedroom, the nighttime cold calmed his harried mind. Stretched out under the linden trees in the gar-den, he tried to imagine what the world might be like beyond the park and the pink house, whose residents came and went, more or less frequently, according to whether they were told or imagined out there in that limitless space populated by human beings. They spoke, sang, told, imagined, and wrote stories: that was all he knew about them. He had always wanted to ask the others what there was beyond the garden surrounded by sky and silence, but his job consisted of seeing and hearing, not asking. During the conversations among his hundreds of brothers and sisters, he picked up phrases that referred to the outside: bedroom, old lady, patient, a child with no appetite, an ill-humored servant, a little girl who couldn't sleep, a schoolyard, a sunny beach, the page of a book, printed letters, teatime, illustrations, rain behind the windowpanes, outings in the country, broken toys, children who cry, adults who remember, women and quarrels, soft voices, men who hit, discordant voices, summer's heat at five in the afternoon on a riverbank . . . It bothered some of his brothers and sisters to be in children's imaginations ("They make you do very strange things and keep you for hours and hours"); they preferred to be in adults' mouths ("They know by heart everything they are going to do with you, they rattle you off and let you go sooner"). The more apathetic ones complained of improvisations: "You get accustomed to being made to do and say more or less the same old thing and suddenly, they change you." But all of them hated to be read; to be condemned to exist in the dead pages of a book, in the form of the printed word, filled them with anguish.

The Ugly Duckling came through the gate; Gretel too. It was dawn when Captain Hook ran down the garden path, putting on his peg leg and cursing the person who was telling him over again that night. Everyone, everyone but him was leaving the pink house; everyone was being told, named, or imagined except *One Left to Tell It*. Sometimes a narrator finished a story by saying "And there was only one left to tell it," but he didn't tell anything about *One Left to Tell It,* condemned to be an eternal observer of everything that happened around him so he could tell it at the appropriate moment, when the story he was living ended, and only he was left to tell it. And what if no one asked him for it? What if no one were interested in everything written in his mind since the beginning? Besides, he asked himself—

and he did not know whether to blame the early daylight or his awareness of the trap of his destiny for the sadness that filled his eyes with tears—, to whom could he tell the story of everyone living here and everything that happened, if he alone were left? He alone, *One Left to Tell It.* No, he would never unload the weight of pictures, memories, anecdotes, stories he dragged around; the dead weight implacably tied him to he knew not what. That drunken boat—his memory, he himself—would keep on sailing in the same circle forever and ever, more and more drunk, never managing to reach the coast or to sink at last. That was his life. Life? He didn't even live; observe and listen, watch others' lives. What did they matter to him? What did they matter?

The first rays of the sun brightened the pink color of the house, the green of the trees in the garden; a sheltering calm appeared to be the only presence there. But in fact only unhappiness dwelt in that abode. And he, he was condemned to witness it, to follow it step by step in order to remember and tell it. No, he knew he would never tell anything. When only one was left to tell it, no one would be there to listen. Besides, one would never be left alone there. The others would never die; unhappy or not, they would always exist and always be the same, with no possibility of altering their lives in even the most insignificant detail, imprisoned by the implacable, fatal destiny that joined them all together. They were phrases, names, words, a product of fantasy. And who was he but one more phrase condemned never to tell everything that happened to the others? He longed for death, the only way to free himself from his memory, from the present, and from the future, a three-part monograph more and more like eternity, whose vision pursued him and filled him with dread. Yes, death, but how to find it? Where? How could a phrase kill itself? Impossible: only the one who uttered or thought it had the gift of killing it by silencing it. A phrase can't cross itself out, or forget itself, or silence itself. Nothing, no one, is so deprived of liberty as words, he said to himself, closing his eyes so as not to see, stopping up his ears so as not to hear. But how could he check his thought, stop the growing conviction that he and the other residents of the pink house would always continue existing as they had always existed, as long as someone, in some corner of the world, continued naming them, writing them, remembering them, imagining them? And if people stopped naming them, reading them, thinking them, would there be enough fire in the universe to burn all the books whose dead pages they had been condemned to fill in the form of letters? Oblivion cannot hold all the thoughts that have thought us, he said to himself; it is impossible for the wind to blow all the voices that have uttered us out of the world, beyond its reach.

No, it was not rain that was depositing warm drops of water on his cheeks. Those were not tears springing from his eyes. He opened them and discovered Tom Thumb crying in a bush into which he had climbed. Why hadn't he noticed the boy before? He was lost and didn't know his way home. He stretched out under the linden trees. *Once upon a Time*'s blond curls grew back, he mentally wrote as he looked at the white form of his sister standing with her back to him on the other side of the lake. No, he couldn't see *Once upon a Time*'s face or, consequently, her expression; but because she kept running her hand over the curls on the back of her neck and tugging at the ends of her locks with quick, nervous jerks, *One Left to Tell It* understood: his sister was about to have hysterics.

THE NAIVE MAN

No, of course he didn't know for sure. How could he?

"Well, did she tell you? No? In that case . . . Please! If she hasn't admitted it, you can't know," repeated the stranger, who brought his persistent observations to a close with this infuriating advice: "No, no, no, nothing in the world should make you try to figure out what will happen; especially when it's something like this . . . Come, come, my friend! How can you know, huh?"

From across the table, the anonymous, unsolicited counselor faced him with his blue egg-shaped eyes, whose shape became more and more pronounced as the wait for an answer that was not forthcoming grew longer and longer. Then, as if to show that he had given up on an answer, the stranger shrugged his angular shoulders under the ravaged wool of a baggy gray overcoat. He raised his hands, opened them, and placed the palms on either side of his head, which he bent toward his listener and turned from side to side in a slow oscillatory movement of disapproval; he emitted another "Ah, love, my friend," followed by a barely audible click of the tongue, held in, rather than expelled, by the movement of his thin, dry lips, which twisted slightly into the faint outline of a grimace that remained unfinished, the merest attempt of muscles to translate heaven-knows-what kind of message, which he abandoned so he could start to outline a smile that would in turn be reduced to a mere sketch around the widely spaced teeth, as the man called the waiter, ordered "Two more," and said, extracting a wrinkled bill from his pocket with a nimble, tremulous hand and resting the other hand on the young man's arm to prevent him from carrying out the act the stranger had quickly forestalled: "Allow me; allow me to pay; it's about the only thing experience is good for."

No, losing control would be unforgivable. He would restrain his aggressiveness toward . . . telephone booths, public benches, bars, the condescending expression on the waiters' faces when he asked for the fourth, the tenth telephone token . . . Those things were the causes of his irritability, yes, those and not the presence of the disagreeable stranger. Even though he could see, on the blurry surface of the mirror to their right, that the man seemed little more than a shabby wreck, a bag of bones and alcohol, the stranger was not to blame for the peculiar ill-will that was fast taking possession of his mind. It would be absurd to make the man responsible for the fury that was gripping his jaws, making him clench his teeth and fists in order to control the compulsive quiver that twitched his lips and hands to the rhythm of an unwanted throbbing. And nevertheless . . .

Nevertheless, he must not deceive himself: he was becoming more savage by the minute. Yes, as unjustifiable as it might seem, he became enraged every time this broken-down human being moved his colorless lips ever so slightly to declare with a brazen face, "Oh, what happiness, my friend! At your age, it's impossible to imagine that at my age . . . Love! A strange thing, isn't it? And believe me, the world has changed, the city has changed, people have changed, and I . . . I, well, I know things really haven't changed, but that's the way I feel, thanks to the lucky, unexpected meeting I told you about and . . . of course, naturally, I also know that the other times, on other similar occasions that happened some time ago and seem so remote to me now . . . well, excuse my being so personal, when I was in love with other women, I felt the same way, I had the same wonderful awareness of the world; and I know that once it was gone the exciting feeling of confidence that makes us believe life is on our side changed again into the commonly accepted evidence that hostility thrives all around us; no, I couldn't believe it could happen again, that such a burst of joy could happen again in my life; no, I couldn't believe it, really, my friend, I couldn't, it was impossible, just as now I can't imagine that this new one will end . . . Oh, I don't even want to think about it! But, at any rate, it's very strange, don't you agree?"

Yes, as irrational as it might seem, he deduced that his uneasiness was related to the human disaster endowed with speech who was seated before him. Of course. And he reaffirmed his decision: he must not deceive himself—and, to that end, he needed to cling to those indispensable words *he must,* strong words, as powerful as a trusty steed, which would protect him from any accusation that might erupt in the bar in an effort to trap and judge those apprehensive reactions the stranger was rousing in him. No, losing control would be unforgivable, but it would be equally unforgivable to fake his emotions. And, he told himself, it was necessary to admit it: he himself, always calm and correct in his reactions, peace-loving and tolerant by nature, found himself suddenly and exceptionally angry at the gaunt, harmless man whose courtesy and untidiness were goading him to violence. Yes, he thought, it was impossible not to acknowledge the irrational impulse that was so unfamiliar to him, since by design, he aspired to rule his feelings and ideas by standards of coherence, logic, and a method of thought pure and free of every instinct.

The discomfort caused by the fear of recognizing something similar—slight though it might be—between himself and the sort of irritable angry young men whose company and friendship he had always despised and shunned became a heavy lump in a specific place in his stomach, solidifying into an unpleasant jabbing that he chose to dissolve by draining his glass in a single gulp. But no, rather than dispel the painful spot, the cognac seemed to have irritated it; now it was pushing, rising up from deep within him: it was rage that was growing inside him like the carbonized bones of a prehistoric animal whose bare, blackened claws sprouted from an ancient dead trunk and extended, long and twisted, as if in a grim, urgent demand to satisfy its murderous instinct. A new "Ah, come on, my friend; calm down, there's no reason for alarm, I'm telling you," from the ashen-colored stranger, violently shook the enraged skeleton that was now spreading into his body; but just as it was about to reveal itself with its grasping tentacles eagerly reaching for the emaciated interlocutor, it stopped.

No, he would never forgive himself for losing control. Nevertheless, he forced himself to consider the situation objectively; it was what he usually did, and nothing in his present situation excused him from that. Anyone in his place, that is to say—he went on—any person capable of forming a rigorous, accurate opinion about the pale, large-eared man who was slowly rocking back and forth in his shabby, oversized gray coat—which was, it seemed, draped over a body whose angular, protruding bones were the sole indication of its existence under that cloth, a body . . . Yes, anyone in his place, any person, he repeated to himself, as gifted as he was with a talent for observation free of any prejudice would agree that the stranger's run-down body, on the brink of collapse, was moving weightlessly, as if controlled by flimsy strings. A huge, nearly bald puppet with bulging blue eyes, playing the part of a drunk, he decided. Or, he corrected himself, a person of the most undesirable kind, turned into a puppet. In either case, a slick character. A charlatan. What was the stranger trying to pump from him? The man was not going to get one word, not one more word from him. That was that.

He was surprised by the disagreeable impact of his own voice exclaiming a brusque "That's that!" at the same time as he found himself half out of his seat with his tightly clenched fists pressing on the table. But he felt even more peculiar when he heard his table mate's voice whispering, "Excuse me, I didn't mean . . . well, I didn't mean to annoy you when I said that, in my opinion, love . . . Of course, people often forget—and in this case, I'm talking about myself—people forget, I say, the years and the thoughts they have spent and which have spent them . . . Fancy that! I said 'the years and the thoughts I have spent'! What do you say about that? The years and the thoughts I have spent! Do you understand, my friend? Do you understand now what I said about love a few seconds ago? Do you understand what a different effect being or not being in love can have on the way we are and think? I said 'The years I have spent' when I could have said 'the years that have spent me.' Why? It's very simple: love. If I were not so in love now, believe me, I would be expressing myself as if the years of my life—and that's a long time—had spent me as if they had consumed me, had left me completely devastated. Ah, time! And how fragile, how fickle is our relationship with the changes that affect us most, isn't that so? A few days ago, scarcely a month, if we had been chatting like friends in this very spot, in this very bar, at this very table, as we are doing right now, I probably would have been telling you that time is a trained army of savage, cruel years that sweep over us, plundering us and our thoughts; and nothing good, no lofty sentiment grows back in our mind. And the fact is that a month ago, I hadn't discovered . . . well, you can understand why I hesitate at my age to keep repeating the words *in love.* Now, on the other hand, time, the years I have been leaving behind seem to me like a series of landscapes I have crossed, varied, differing landscapes embellished by people who used to live there, that I met in passing; people and scenery like . . . from another country, that's it, as if they made up the physical and human scenery of a far-off country to which I traveled unexpectedly for a reason I don't remember and where I stayed longer than expected but, in any case, which I left on a return trip that must have taken a very long time, because, although it's hardly been a month since I left that remote country I call my life, it seems as if years have gone by, because what I saw and experienced there strikes me as very muddled. I don't know if, at your age, you can understand what I mean . . . You will forgive how poorly I'm explaining the feeling of not being able to locate those cityscapes and emotional scenes that represent my past, or to recognize myself in the person who passed through them, the person I used to be and who now . . . Odd, don't you agree? I say odd because I never left this city and theoretically, I should have no knowledge of that feeling of empty time between two far-apart places that settles in the mind of the person who, they say, suddenly moves from one place to another—by plane, for example . . . But that wasn't exactly what I was trying to tell you; but . . . Ah, yes! No, I wasn't trying to

annoy or offend you when I tried to explain that, in my opinion, love . . ."

Yes, yes, yes, he must make an effort and manage to calm
down. Yes, yes, yes, he must breathe deeply, stretch his muscles,
try to relax even if it means withholding his honest opinion. He
mustn't say it. He mustn't say it. He mustn't say it. And much
better than revealing—in view of his sincere nature and his
aversion even to white lies—yes, much better to abstain from
any opinion than to reveal the justifiable opinion he had formed
of the stranger. And to that end he resolved not to listen, not to
listen to the grotesque charlatan. Let the charlatan talk by himself, he decided. The man's filthy wordiness would not soil him.
"You poor idiot," he mentally fired at him. How the stranger
chattered, assuming that he had chanced upon a pleasant con-
versationalist. He was less than two feet away from the stranger;
he kept his face expressionless—although he did see that it was
tense when he looked out of the corner of his eye at the mirror,
peeling in spots, to his right—and wrapped in a self-imposed
coldness against which each and every one of the stranger's
words would shatter. The coldness would not flag for an instant
in its appointed task: to spew, spew, spew out the most total
and absolute indifference through every pore of the skin on his
hardened face.

He looked straight at the dandruff-flecked stranger with such
a still, hard gaze, he thought—and his thought contained no
self-reproach, only a self-assured, invigorating pride at having
managed to adopt, once and for all, the unyielding expression
he now displayed—yes, a gaze so still and hard that it was starting to cause a hint of pain in the eyes from which it was ema-
nating. But his gaze, which was meant to erect blocks of scorn,
instead let a part of itself escape surreptitiously through the corner of his eye, allowing him to look at the right-hand wall and
see himself in the mirror, which was filthy like the rest of the
place.

The fastidiousness that was obviously the essential note of his
own image reached him from the mirror like a cool breeze to

soothe the tension built up during the recent hours. Of course, he wasn't in the least surprised by his spotless appearance or the meticulous arrangement of his outward presence, since they were customary in him. But confirming the impeccable line of his white suit, the absence of wrinkles in his pants and coat, the scrupulous arrangement of collar and tie despite the absurdity that had burst into his life exactly five hours and forty minutes ago, calmed his anxiety and even . . .

He felt as if all the blood in his body had rushed to his head, which was about to burst. Surely an exaggerated reaction, he admitted. But the stain was there. Not, as he had first supposed, on the surface of the mirror, which was grimy like the rest of the bar, including the waiters and clientele, not to mention the revolting stranger. The stain was on his shirt cuff, and it was from cognac. A sign of unheard-of carelessness in him, a person who was abstemious out of deep ethical conviction. That slovenly individual, yes, that slovenly individual had persuaded him to drink. Why, he wondered indignantly, since they were not acquainted, had the stranger sat down across from him, with his hypocritical "Am I disturbing you? No? In that case, allow me, it's not good to drink alone; no, no, it isn't good, when one is young like you." And the man had taken a seat there, at his table, even though there were other tables, whose enviably unoccupied and solitary condition made the limited space in the bar look empty rather than full.

They made it look empty. The thought of it produced an unlocatable distaste that at first was dispersed and generalized throughout his body, until he later noticed it had become limited and concrete, concentrated in a certain zone of his palate affected by a negative gustatory factor that—in acknowledgement of the overwhelming nervousness of the moment—he counteracted with another large cognac. But, as he thought about what he had thought (that the revolting solitary tables in that revolting bar seemed to make the place look empty rather than full), a violent fury against the man before him was added to the distaste that now entirely controlled his feelings.

The thought about the goddamned chairs was not his own. Never, he said to himself, had his mind gotten lost along the paths of emptiness and inanity. Never, he repeated to himself. He had never found himself thinking nonsense. It was in that other head, nodding condescendingly as it repeated, "Ah, my friend, love, love," where illogical random chance was plotting out irrational thoughts. It was the intruder, not he, who had thought, "They make it look empty," the intruder—why hadn't he noticed it before, at the very instant the stranger set the trap for him? Yes, it was the intruder who had thought it and had even done so aloud and perhaps on purpose—yes, on purpose—to try to confuse him, him, a mild, orderly, methodical, and peaceful citizen, who—no—would not lose control, would not bash in the man's head. He had never wanted to bash in anyone's head. Never. Anyone who said otherwise was a liar. Anyone who dared to impute the slightest hint of aggressiveness to him was insulting him grievously. Insulting? No, even worse: it would mean trying to distort his personality, an intolerable maliciousness for which he would find an appropriate response.

Of course, he asserted: an appropriate response. If that charlatan, who was repeating to him again, "Will you allow me to give you some advice? Wait, wait; don't rush. A woman in love may not always act as we would wish or foresee, but that doesn't mean she isn't truly in love"—yes, if that lying charlatan dared to assert, merely insinuate that he had ever in his life felt aggressive urges toward anyone, if those stammering lips dared to express such an insult, he would certainly lose control and be obliged to bash in that egg-shaped face, a very large gray egg, he said to himself, with two smaller blue eggs under thin, long, arched brows—too arched, he concluded. Brows like that, he decided contemptuously, were an expression of perpetual surprise, as if life for such a person were like watching a parade of surprises, a cavalcade of oddities; as if he thought that in order to be granted the right of observer all he needed was the expression of amazement that exempts the person who displays it from taking any action. That attitude was what exasperated him so.

He would eliminate individuals of that kind, like the man who was staring at him with the pair of eggs whose blue yolks seemed about to burst open and spill down his cheeks onto the table, dirtying it with all the vile things they had ever seen — he would gladly eliminate them from any public setting that claimed to have minimal hygienic, moral, and inspirational conditions for humanity. Passive individuals, loafers who preached, "Be patient, calm down. Another drink? Allow me . . ." and who imputed aggressive motives to those who take any action in the immovable, alien landscape into which such people's cowardly, impotent amazement had turned their lives. Yes, he reassured himself, he would remove such people, and not aggressively, as that coward in front of him might believe. Did the stranger believe such a thing? Had he said so? He, aggressive? He? In the face of such an insult, he grasped the edge of the table with both hands to control the force driving him to attack the stranger. He must breathe deeply, relax his arms on the table, his thighs on the chair, his feet on the floor. No, he couldn't lose control. People find out about everything, they know everything in a city as small as his, where he lived and must continue to live. He must not allow himself illogical, unsuitable actions that could damage him when people gossiped about them. And, to tell the truth, it would be illogical to attack the man with intent to harm, because he had not said anything insulting. And after all, one had to admit that he might be right. How could he know? How could he know whether she. . . ?

No, it was impossible to be sure or even to assume. Because, as the stranger was repeating once again, "If she hasn't given you the slightest hint, if there hasn't been the remotest threat . . ." How could there have been? They had not spoken. He had spent more than two hours trying to communicate with her by telephone. He would ask the waiter for another telephone token. No, the waiter disgusted him. As a general rule, he loathed waiters. They moved slowly and mechanically behind the counter and looked around from time to time as if the stage set of the bar, barely animated by the colorless walk-ons who were its clients, were the world, the only world possible, and as if, resigned to their wretched fate, they could be only what they were: waiters. He loathed them. He would not ask the waiter for any more tokens. It got on his nerves: the waiter's manner of appearing indifferent but, at the same time, secure in the deep conviction—surely, he thought, surely that's the way the waiter feels—of knowing everything that happened inside the four public walls and of understanding the reasons the paltry number of nighttime customers talked to each other there and not somewhere else.

But the waiter could not fool him. Even pretending to be sleepy, despite the tired motion with which he was drying the glassware and the slow, almost accidental way he looked in his direction, the waiter revealed the condescension peculiar to a person who thinks he knows the secret invisible mechanism that prompts events and the actions of men around them. The waiter, who was refilling his glass at the request of the scrawny stranger, surely thought—as did all in his despicable profession, he said to himself—that those dim premises were the whole universe and that this universe was governed according to physical laws required by the listless fiddling with glasses, bottles, wet cloths and by the infrequent entrances and exits of men and women whose lives the waiter thought he knew. Yes, he thought, like all of them, that the waiter believes that the world is his establishment, humanity his customers, and that he knows by heart what is happening, has happened, and will happen, what the temporary inhabitants of the place are like and their innermost thoughts, passions, and shabbiness. A filthy world he thinks he knows with his eyes shut, as if it were a matter of a closed book whose contents he has memorized by dint of handling it so often. An abominably written book, he told himself, on low-grade paper, poorly bound, which the waiter has read so many times that he needs only to give a quick glance at the person entering the premises to know the page and chapter to which the character belongs. That's why the waiter was looking at him, to put him in his appropriate place in the great book of his monotonous, greasy experience. He felt himself being pulled from his seat by the waiter's cataloguing look, which would drag him away and then drop him into the insipid pages of the dead book of his dishwasher's mind: he would be forever imprisoned between the covers with no possibility of correcting the slanderous writing into which his person had been translated.

"If you touch me, I'll . . ." Had he heard correctly? Was that his voice? Were those his hands that had pounced on the glass, his the fingers that encircled and squeezed it hard like an imaginary neck he would like to wring? Yes, it was he, he must have been the one who exclaimed, "If you lay a hand on me, I'll. . . ," to judge by the voice that uttered those words and that he recognized as his own, and by the astonishment of the stranger, who opened the blue eggs of his eyes as wide as he could and gave him a look . . . Oh no, not that! That's all I need, he thought; because the stranger's eyes had the glassy, pink, moist look that heralds the flow of tears. And although the bulging ovals did not release a single drop of the slippery fluid he saw filling them, the mere thought that it could happen disgusted him almost as much as feeling on his arm the bony grayish hand of the stranger who was trying to encourage him by pressing into his arm his long fingers with dirty, peeling nails. "I know the feeling, believe me. But that's all it is—a feeling. No one will lay a hand on you, my friend. No one. Don't be afraid. You have no reason to be, really. I understand what kind of disturbance is troubling your mind. That feeling of worthlessness and the hostility we perceive around us combine to overwhelm us when we imagine that everything is over. I know, I know; I have gone through it. And I share your anguish. But look: I said 'I have gone through it.' Why? Because it's temporary, so temporary that I would be lying if I told you I went through it only once. There have been so, so many . . . But calm down, my friend. Calm down. Because, one day—Bam! Everything turns around, everything changes, and a transition takes place that saves us . . . things, people, life in general seem as if they are showing us their other face, the friendly one. And everything turns around here, here, yes, up here," the man repeated, tapping his forehead with his index finger. "Since everything takes place up here, let's suppose," and he tapped his forehead again with his index finger, "let's suppose she appears through that door. Because although everything happens up here, the sign comes from without—yes—and that's the great misfortune, my friend: symbols belong to the outside world; they are the outside world, that forest of signs where the power of our dreams is useless . . . But let's suppose, as I was saying, she appears through that door, or that later, or tomorrow, you and she talk and clear up your misunderstanding. Because usually there is some misunderstanding about schedules or words or gestures; and according to what you have told me, and pardon my insistence, it can't be a question of anything that could shatter the special happiness, that . . . Oh, my friend, while you experience that rapture that makes us walk along the streets reconciled with the idea that the world does exist, and the sun shining through the leaves of the trees is a brand-new sun we had never noticed before . . ."

"What sun? What leaves? What trees?" he wondered in his mind. "What sun? What leaves? What trees?" his thought repeated insistently to blot out the voice of the intruder. "What sun? What leaves? What trees?" he heard himself mutter, trying to interrupt the senseless discourse of his table mate who exclaimed, "What do you mean, what sun, what leaves, what trees?" and then ordered, "Two more cognacs, doubles, please," doubtless to accompany the forthcoming answer with which he was euphorically promising himself to resolve the triple question. But scarcely had the greenish large-eared egg that was his face come closer, and before the stranger had begun to speak, he heard the splutter of his own voice repeating with deliberate and increasing rudeness, "What sun? What leaves? What trees?" Now he interrupted himself because, standing by the table, serving them two double cognacs, was the object of his recent flash of hatred. And as he relaxed his tense back against the back of the chair, he discovered he no longer held a grudge against the waiter.

The forgiveness, spontaneously granted in such a generous way that he wasn't even aware of when or why he had given it, acted on him like a drug prescribed as a sedative that in an overdose induces restlessness closer to anguish than to the sought-after relief. Suddenly freed from the distinctly unpleasant duty of having to maintain his disapproval of an individual who was—for he held fast in his opinion regarding the waiter—nothing but a mercenary of vice and crime after dark, he initially felt he was going to unwind at last; but as his contracted muscles relaxed, they continued beyond the desired level of slackness, and he ended up feeling the overwhelming giddiness of physical collapse. And what was perhaps worse: the mental obliteration that such a collapse brought with it, a state associated with defeat—or with disorientation, which is the same thing, he thought—a state, he knew, that generally followed a change in his ideas or emotions. Since those changes tended to make him feel more lenient, they confronted him with an upsetting question: was that leniency due to an error of reason or an excess of generosity?

Why had his sensitivity—not his reason, he corrected—suddenly acquitted the waiter? He no longer felt angry at the unfortunate dishwasher. But the glory—he had to admit it, he thought—belonged to him alone, not to the waiter; the triumph was his, his, for having managed to remain calm and collected as befitted his temperament and character, before the underling, or owner, of that seedy bar, who continued to stand by the table, wearing a short jacket whose original white color was now distinctly grayish green, with skimpy, wrinkled lapels and frayed cuffs and sagging pockets. The scrawny knot on his discolored black tie was so loose that it revealed the missing button on the narrow shirt collar with its curled, yellowish points, and his enormous Adam's apple—a greasy protruberance like a chicken's rump, he observed—was covered with the prickly black stubble and flaking skin that a bad shave spread over the rest of his neck and his chin.

Standing, leaning on the table with a hand that surely belonged to the porcine species—he judged, draining the glass
again—the waiter was speaking familiarly with the stranger,
while turning toward him from time to time the suspicious
look of his tiny, dull eyes, half-closed under the weight of puffy
lids and thick, frowning brows. Why tolerate some menial in a
bar eying him distrustfully? No, he would not be the one to lose
his temper and dirty his hands by hitting that greasy, dishonest
face. However, why put up with suspicious looks from a criminal? Yes, he said to himself, a criminal. And, if not a criminal,
certainly the accomplice of other criminals. What, if not nefari-
ous reasons, would link the manager of that pigsty with the
squalid stranger who had been pestering him all night long with
the story of his life? They were talking with a familiarity not created in a day. They certainly knew each other. For days, many
days. Did I say days? For nights, many nights, he deduced triumphantly, because that kind of human rat only stirred and
came out in the dark of night. A regular, of course, the ashen
man with the egg face had to be a regular. A regular—of what, if
not debauchery and crime?

He did not hear what they were saying. He had managed to
become deaf to the words of this sex maniac who talked about
nothing but women. Although the man had exclaimed, "Ah,
love," he knew perfectly well to what kind of love he was referring. The only kind that could take place between vagrants and
prostitutes. He didn't hear what they were saying. Fortunately,
he thought, because merely seeing them made him shake with
spasms of nausea, almost to the point of vomiting, he said to
himself, which surely would have been inevitable if he had
heard the words of that pair of social rejects. At any rate, although the words of the conversation came to him as if from
very far away, he didn't have to be overshrewd to imagine the
waiter's involvement. Otherwise, why did he treat a customer
who would have been kicked out of any respectable establishment so affably, even with a certain inexplicable protectiveness?
No, he must not tolerate that exhibition of coordinated cynicism

before him. Nor would he forgive himself for losing control. But between the two positions, between leaping at the throats of those two conspirators or witnessing with indifference their shameless perversion, there was—or there should have been, he specified—an intermediate attitude that would seem dignified both to himself and to others. Because the first option, that is, losing control, would mean—however right he may have been, and he was sure of being so, completely—giving an opportunity to the town gossip, who, he knew only too well, was looking for the chance to spread all kinds of falsehoods about his person that would be highly detrimental to his reputation. As soon as he committed the slightest error, even the air that he was breathing so free and easy, would become an ally of that urban vermin and would carry from ear to ear with euphoric determination all the calumnies treacherously concocted against him. Attacking the waiter . . . No, impossible. He must not. But adopting the opposite position, that is, witnessing their intrigues . . . No, not that either. And it was his duty to make it very clear that he, he would not consent . . . Without violence—although he had more than enough reasons to exercise it, he admitted to himself—without scandal, he would overpower the two malefactors neatly, forcefully. Yes, he would overpower them. With words, that was the right way, a praiseworthy course of action, he said to himself. He would strike them down by shooting a clear, incisive speech at them. Boldly, he continued; yes, he would talk to them as if he were shooting. He would discharge at them the most deadly of all weapons: the truth. The truth about the dunghill of their lives. It was a right and a civic duty to prevent the twisted projects of those two feverish minds from becoming acts with unpredictable consequences. And dangerous, he added.

A long swallow of cognac made the bitter retching, which was moving up from his stomach and pushing at his throat as it tried to leave his body, descend again to its place of origin. He shivered. He breathed deeply several times and opened his eyes. The mirror to his right had stopped swaying, but his own image was wavering on the surface. On the other hand, he thought he could distinguish perfectly the shiftless waiter's tiny eyes under the puffy eyelids. He had fled for protection behind the counter. Did the waiter fear his words? Had the waiter escaped without giving him the chance to tell him off? Why had he spared the waiter instead of punishing him verbally yet severely? His own evident inclination toward forgiveness disgusted him. He knew he was generous, but it bothered him that his characteristic lack of malice might be confused with the inveterate capacity for self-deception in people who believe they have forgiven but in reality are resorting to a grotesque, childish ruse: excusing their own shortcomings in others. Isn't what they call forgiveness just a cover-up for expediency and cowardice? he said to himself. That "to err is human," a phrase to which they resort at the time of forgiveness — wasn't it a shield people brandished to protect and, in addition, to hide their own imperfection and to make of this world, which they appear to understand by the act of absolving it, an immense garbage dump where they can have a place? Ah, no, he admitted to himself, draining the glass, in him there was no baseness by virtue of which he could make common cause with the waiter or owner of that bar or whatever he was . . . No. Nevertheless, he no longer felt angry at the individual, in spite of having serious arguments to prove that he was from the lowest human category. No, the waiter didn't annoy him, no matter how much he tried to enumerate the arguments in his mind. A useless attempt, on the other hand. Because the arguments escaped him; they fled from his thought like fragments of an interior landscape composed with intellectual balance and suddenly blown away by an ill wind: inanity. Because the wind that was suddenly penetrating the half-closed door of his mind and was carrying off the arguments and reasons he had so patiently and logically worked out was the voice of his table mate.

"Forgiveness, you say? How can you be surprised that in the end you always forgive? It's normal in your condition," the voice — of the stranger? — reached him. Yes, although less halting than in its previous interruptions and somewhat triumphant, it was the voice of that man, who suddenly lifted his head, raised the upper part of a skeleton one would have sworn was broken, and captured his attention, compelling him to look into extraordinarily large eyes that were so blue, he thought, they almost moved him. He could not stop looking at them. Everything spun around him when he tried to deflect the gaze of those eyes whose brightness infused a peculiar transparency through the stranger's oval face, which seemed made of celluloid at that moment. If those eyes, which were getting bigger and bigger, ended up by bursting, he feared, if those eyes, overflowing with so much brilliance, exploded, if those eyes touched him with their luminous blue, he would be fatally wounded, he told himself.

"Of course you forgive, my friend. And why? Ah me!" he sighed, lifting his bony shoulders. And he put the palms of his hands on either side of his head. "Why? Why? When he loves, man is a sun who sees everything and transfigures everything. At least, those are the words of a poet who was known as the Madman in his time. He also said that man is a god when he dreams and a beggar when he thinks. I believe—and I do not mean to attain the loftiness of that great expert on things human and divine—I believe, as I say—and forgive me if I seem opinionated—I believe it is true. And if we replace *dreams* with *loves,* which, in my humble opinion, is the same thing, because everything, everything happens up here"—and he tapped his forehead insistently with his index finger—"yes, here, up here; so, it is not less true that man is a god when he loves and a beggar when he thinks, that is to say, when he does not love. Because, what thoughts about the world and its affairs can a man in love frame? None. Impossible. Before he falls in love, yes, and afterwards, too, once he is hurt and miserable because he is no longer in love. But while . . . Oh, no! While we dwell in the immensity of the rapturous feeling that makes us immense, we can't measure it with the same yardstick and by standards we apply to the analysis of everything else, that is to say, of the petty, wretched, in short, measurable or 'thinkable' part of life and of ourselves, portions or aspects of existence to which,

unfortunately, we do pay attention when we see ourselves expelled from the measureless expanse that is love and in which
you now have the good fortune to dwell. So your forgiveness is
inevitable; clemency flows uncontrollably from you: you have
now turned into a god with no authority over the degrees of
perfection or of baseness of those who . . . Oh, how unhappy
others seem to us, all those around us who do not know or have
lost the sacred feeling of being immersed in the harmony that
joins without binding all that is good and beautiful in life, right?
The good? The bad? The wicked? The noble? The despicable?
They never give up lying in wait for us with questions; they urge
us to think about something or someone. And we can't, my
friend. No. Because—surely the same thing is happening to
you—you can't avoid considering yourself different when you
are in love. Different, I say. Not better or worse, value judg-
ments that don't even cross our minds, but just different and—
how can I say it?—yes, and a little inconsiderate with regard to
others. I will try to explain that feeling of revulsion and also of
inability to judge, even when we must judge someone, the feeling that leads us, when people point out a fellow who at present
is terribly pessimistic, to ask ourselves, Who knows what he
used to be like, sometime in the more or less distant past, when
he felt that very same way of being in the world that inspires us
today and is characterized, at least in my opinion, by content-
ment and reconciliation with the idea of existing. . . ? Yes, we
can't help thinking about what beautiful things that person
might have contained then, for, no matter how much we think
otherwise, we can't judge him now because we barely know
him; we don't know what he's like, because one would say that,
since he is without the love we so fortunately enjoy, he belongs
to another species. Don't you think so?"

No, no, forget about "we." He had never, ever had any of those
hysterical experiences; he—and he wanted to leave the matter
properly settled once and for all—never ever felt, thought,
imagined, or even in his worst nightmares dreamed anything
that even remotely hinted at something in common with this

carnival charlatan. Neither he nor Laura—in spite of the foolish behavior of "your fiancée," as the tavern rat who was facing him called her—neither he nor Laura bore any relation to the unwholesome union of this drunkard with his prostitute. Who but a prostitute in complete physical, moral, and economic decay would be capable of having a carnal relationship with such a ridiculous man? Insanity, nothing but insanity was concealed in the saloon oratory with which the man was trying to establish a similarity between their love lives.

"Insanity, nothing but insanity," he repeated aloud now, because now he was certainly going to tell the stranger everything, everything he thought about his dirty . . . But the words, the thought that joined them together, the idea, the four essential, emphatic ideas on which he would base the truth, the whole truth that the man deserved and that he was going to spit in his face right now—but he couldn't, he couldn't speak because they slipped away, flying, escaping into the distance, over the tables in the bar, over the sleep-distorted faces of the half dozen clients. The conclusions at which he had arrived rose, ascended toward the ceiling of the establishment, and were then lost in the darkness at the back of the barroom, to reappear broken into phrases, into words that floated in the cigarette fumes and alcohol vapors; they fell on the bar, bounced, hit the waiter full in the face, then smashed into the array of bottles lined up behind the counter. No, impossible to get up, to run after his fugitive thought and recover it instead of allowing it to become saturated with an atmosphere that prevented him from breathing, from standing up, and nimbly, quickly catching everything he had worked out to say: there it was, ambling from one side to another, now at a dizzying speed, now with the slow rhythm of weightlessness. He was unable to seize it, and not one person there supported him by trying to help him with his task, something that was now impossible, unrealizable because he was trying to overcome his choking by breathing deeply and allowing himself to be handled by the waiter and the stranger, who were loosening his tie and unbuttoning his shirt, while he, with a misinterpreted, clumsy gesture of his hand, insistently pointed at the peeling walls, down which he saw something slide: those truths that he felt it his duty to utter aloud and that would never be the same again, soiled during the disgraceful stroll that was soon to end when they perished, hopelessly stuck to depressing postcard views of European capitals in shrill Technicolor.

"Take it easy, take it easy. There, that's it, lean against the back of the chair, good, that way, that's it. Let your arms relax on the table. Unclench your fists. Exactly. See? Nothing is wrong, absolutely nothing." The stranger's long fingers struggled with his hands, forcing him to keep his fingers spread open on the table.

A strong, bitter taste in his mouth and the near impossibility of moving his swollen tongue, stuck to the dry roof of his mouth, were the first sensations to which he awoke. "Drink, my friend, drink. It will do you good." The retching, which rose to his throat as soon as the smell of the coffee reached him, stopped after he swallowed the liquid. And then, under the effect of the spasm that convulsed him entirely, he noticed that the unpleasant bitterness he had localized on the curd-speckled roof of his mouth didn't come exclusively from his taste buds, which reported to him concerning the rotten state of the internal zones of his person; it also came from the olfactory nerves that, like a merciless antenna, called to his attention the fermented evidence displayed on his exterior person, the natural, material result of nausea and heaving—and fresh, as indicated by his body's memory, which he had regained after swallowing the coffee—in the form of yellowish and greenish stains that dampened and stiffened part of his shirt and white flannel suit.

Don't look at yourself in the mirror was the first order dictated by his will, which he recovered after the momentary blackout. It was enough to run his hand clumsily over his damp, uncombed hair and to see the front of his suit wrinkled and covered with vomit to understand that, in fact, he must avoid at all cost the image that the mirror would send back should he look at himself in it. His right hand, unsure but urgent, felt the inside pocket of his jacket. Yes, his wallet was still there. And, a little ashamed of his distrustful gesture but unable to repress its instinctive repetition, he did the same thing with the back pocket of his pants, obtaining an identical and reassuring result. Everything in order. This verification restored to him not only the assurance that he still had on his person what, moments before, he feared had been removed, but also part of the lost knowledge of what happened. Because the only thing he remembered about the period of time of which he wasn't fully aware was having felt overcome by terror and distrust. A vague memory he could now confirm in the fleeting pictures in which he was the central figure, like a cheap collection of ineptly photographed, poorly developed postcards that his memory ran quickly across the torn screen of his mind, causing him to remember himself stumbling in the middle of the bar, to see once more how the stranger and the waiter held him up, one on each arm, and led him to a door that wasn't properly closed and that he was afraid to enter, because he didn't know what he would find instead of the toilet, the toilet, the toilet that the waiter so insistently announced and that he so persistently rejected, putting one hand on the pocket where he kept his wallet, since he was so certain they were dragging him to some disgusting hole where he would be the object of robbery and physical violence or in which they would try to involve him in the corrupt machinations of the prostitute, about whom the man in the gray overcoat had spoken to him throughout the entire evening, in order to subject him later to the vilest blackmail. He remembered his fear, which he now realized was unfounded, but not what had happened to make the two men practically run with him to the toilet, or why the waiter, with a particularly serious and respectful voice, called the untidy character with the egg-shaped face "professor," or much less why the latter, the stranger, managed to inspire in him—him—an unexpected feeling of safety and admiration—while he was dragging him forcibly toward where he was refusing to go—by simply repeating almost gracefully, "Don't worry, my friend. Allow me, allow me to help you, that's the only thing experience as extensive as mine is good for."

Even knowing it was now an unnecessary movement, he returned his still-trembling hand to his jacket pocket to feel the
presence of his wallet. He breathed deeply, just as the cynically
nicknamed "professor" on the other side of the table was advis-
ing him to do. And to his present shame was added a forebod-
ing of the disgust that the picture—also of himself—would recall on the following day; the spectacle she had caused him to
make of himself as a result of stupid incidents like the one that
took place that afternoon; the picture of himself as an evening
customer in the bar, located opposite the entrance to the house
where she lives, searching for telephone tokens or waiting for
her to get the idea that he was expecting her to appear there; the
one of himself in his impatience, consuming drinks that under
normal conditions—that is, when she doesn't let the foolish
side of her personality take over—he never imbibes; the one in
which he is the main character, going back and forth uncontrollably from the bar to the telephone and from the telephone
to the bar until the contemptuous expression of the waiter
pushes him to a table, the one in the back of the room, the farthest from the telephone and the bar, the one most remote
from the instrument that is the witness and object of his nervous perseverance. She, she had driven him to alcoholic intoxi-
cation, he told himself, she and that inveterate drunk who kept
on making a speech with a total lack of inhibition: "I'll tell you
that, contrary to what people usually think, experience is not a
form of wisdom, it implies no accumulation of knowledge, and
it is not even a good counselor. It isn't wise, or strengthening, or
prudent; it isn't even farsighted. Believe me, my friend, experience is only a form of nostalgia. Nostalgia for a past in which
time was something that still had not begun to run out and that
we suddenly remember because someone around us also feels
that way, and we recognize ourselves in that person amazed at
the passage of time. But such recognition implies no value judgment about our past behavior or the behavior of the person
who reminds us of it, and it does not imply considerations
about what it might have been and wasn't, what we could have

avoided and didn't. It is simply like glancing at the face of someone fixed in a yellowing photo and saying, yes, I was that person, someone whose image the years would yellow. It's a matter
of a simple act of recognition and nostalgia, nothing more. And
I'll tell you, that very experience—which did not help us to
know ourselves, or to know others better, or to improve ourselves, or to correct ourselves, or to avoid wrongdoing against
ourselves or others, because time is the only experience we do
accumulate—that experience is at best useful, I say, only in cases
like the present one, in which the person whose situation brings
back to us the memory of old feelings is a friend, and then we
do allow ourselves to tell him: forget, forget this morbid vision
of your present condition as soon as possible, because it is an
erroneous vision, a hallucination produced by the fears we
sometimes take for reality even when we are happy. And believe
me, happiness is fragile, and if we allow its surroundings to be
infiltrated by visions of unhappiness, however illusory they may
be, it eventually deteriorates. Forget, forget what has happened.
A young man like yourself, intelligent, brilliant, with subtle feelings, so humane and understanding, motivated by the purest
disinterest to engage in such a noble profession—a profession
between science and art, a frontier where very few minds can
create—a person so . . . so . . . and you must excuse my frankness,
so sensitive, so extremely sensitive, needs to sacrifice part of his
noble sentiments in his own defense. Because those fears . . .
Come, come! How can you allow yourself to suspect something
she hasn't even hinted at?"

How true, he thought, he certainly was like that: intelligent,
sensitive—too sensitive, as the stranger had described him—
generous, devoted to a profession that borders on both art and
science, which demanded an orderliness, a precision of life and
thought that at times—and here's where the problem lay, he
said to himself, having now recovered from his recent indispo-
sition—Laura could not understand or make an effort to respect.
And on such occasions, yes—he admitted it—when Laura's un-
conventional ways altered the strict rules of his methodical enterprise, he lost control.

Incidents like today's had occurred before. She would say, I'll call or I'll wait downstairs at eight. And a little before eight, the attack of doubt would begin: should he wait downstairs or by the telephone? And he would go up and down, from the street to the telephone and from the telephone to the street, for a span of time that went on and on, not knowing whether Laura's non-appearance was the result of a delay concerning the hour of arrival or of telephoning, or if she had arrived below just when he had gone up to see whether she had telephoned, or if she had telephoned just as he had gone down to the street in case she had arrived to pick him up.

I'll call at eight o'clock or I'll wait downstairs, she had said. No, that was no way to do things, no matter how insistently the tedious stranger qualified Laura's vagueness as "trifles, trifles. What's important, what's really important is that, when you overcome these trifles, then . . . Ah, love!" No, he could not expose his sensitivity to situations as tense as this one—and the stranger was correct in that regard—which wasn't going to reach the disastrous climax that his overexcitement had made him fear a few hours earlier. To shake off any intimation of a threat on her part, it was enough for him to remember—now having regained his habitual composure after the distressing gastric upset—that on previous occasions Laura had eventually found him there, in that very bar located opposite the entrance to her house, to Laura's house, which was, actually, contrary to what his frequently dreadful memory had noted, the place where they were supposed to meet, though he had the time wrong also. An error he might have made again, he thought, suddenly recalling past misunderstandings, as he consulted his appointment book where, in fact, he found the proof of his own confusion.

A ridiculous, but forgivable, confusion, he said to himself, and one that Laura would be able to understand without the need for long explanations, unlike the nincompoop who was trying to delay him with words and stories that had nothing to do with him. "Remember that man is a god when he loves and a beggar when he thinks. How else can you explain the mystery of believing blindly, each time you fall in love, that the marvelous woman you love and the wonderful bond with the world that sums up your life aren't the projection of something present only within you but are something real? The human ability to believe, in the presence of something wonderful, in the presence of love, that we have discovered it and it appears to be something new, when in reality it is a matter of a relapse, is very naive. How naive! Don't you agree? How naive! But how beautiful, isn't it? And how necessary for it to happen that way, even if it's only once in a while. Yes, I see that you share my opinion."

Naive? Naive? What, he asked himself, could that swindler know about any noble sentiment? Nevertheless, his even-tempered and generous nature has finally asserted itself—as always, he thought—and really, he did feel rather sorry for the man, sprawled on the floor with a split lip and a bloody nose, whom he had no other choice but to hit so he could leave the bar where the stranger insisted on delaying him under the pretext of not allowing him to do anything rash.

He had reason enough, he told himself, to have acted with violence and in legitimate self-defense. He was pleased, however, to confirm that he had not been wrong in his estimate of the man with the egg-shaped face and gray overcoat: he was undoubtedly a lying charlatan. At least, that was implied in the words of the waiter, who ran to help the stranger as he lay on the floor and was saying as he wiped off the blood flowing from his nose and mouth, "Fantasy, professor, more fantasy."

He didn't understand the meaning of the words that followed, which he heard almost in the doorway. "Why do you invent kind-hearted stories to buck up some baby-faced fool who quarrels with his girlfriend, gets drunk because he can't hold his liquor, and can't even go to the toilet by himself to piss? It's always the same! You'd do better to look out for yourself, professor. Tell me now, who is going to buck you up. . . ?" Nor did he understand how that dishonest-looking person, still sitting on the floor, beaten and unmasked, had the gall to look toward the door through which he was leaving and, still trying to defend his actions to the waiter, say with an astonished expression, full of amazement and surprise, "No, no, they are not stories, not kind-hearted stories, because everything, everything that's true happens here, here," he repeated tapping his forehead with his index finger.

And now in the street, after the slam of the door, he did not hear and he did not want to hear more. And he began to run, contrary to his customary sedateness, a habit he broke because of the urgency of his need to go home, take a relaxing, cooling bath, change his suit, and regain his usual composure, in order to get to the theater exit where he was to see Laura, according to the engagement he had jotted down in the appointment book in his own handwriting. A meeting at which he would be loathe to arrive late. But sometimes unpunctuality, so rare in him, was unavoidable, he told himself, because of the complications that Laura's mixed-up schedules and activities caused in his daily routine.

THE PROBLEM

In the course of their complex and difficult existence, all Problems in the world suffer from intense crises of anguish, read the Problem, lying in bed. He was not reclining; instead, his shoulders and head seemed to have collapsed onto huge pillows whose bright pink color accentuated the pallor of his face, the dark circles under his eyes, and the sunken cheeks still damp with traces of recent weeping.

The affected Problem, the Problem continued to read with considerable effort of his irritated eyes, which struggled to fix their gaze on the dancing signs printed in the book he was trying to hold firmly, although his trembling hands only caused it to shake wildly.

The affected Problem, he read again, *displays unusual pallor and suffers from frightful nightmares. In them, he is analyzed, scrutinized, and finally solved, with boundless indifference and objectivity, by odious analytical minds. He believes he is lost and trapped in a forest of clear, concrete ideas from which he cannot flee. A dreadfully luminous sky, with not a single cloud of doubt, threatens to barrage the earth with streams of lucidity. In such nightmares, the Problem often feels surrounded and pursued by a mob of sensible thoughts capable of seizing him and leading him to his dreaded end with no recourse; the defenseless Problem is dragged before logical judgment, which callously pronounces the sentence. The sentence is inexorable and is carried out. In the tormented sleeper's restless dream, dawn is a festival of white light and limpidity on the beach at the seashore. A dark stain tries unsuccessfully to soil this triumph of total whiteness. Instead, the stain accentuates the whiteness: it is the guilty Problem advancing over the sand, in the midst of a squad formed by the bailiffs of good sense. Imposing, impenetrable as always, the Problem's black figure stands out against a foamy background, and he invokes the*

holy name of his insolubility in vain; in vain he appeals to his eter-
nal consubstantiality with the very being of the universe: the squad
aims and fires flashes of common sense. A third-rate truism pierces
his heart with uncouth accuracy.

The Problem awakens, seized with horror and bathed in cold
sweat. No matter how hard he tries to calm down or how often he
repeats over and over that he is still alive and insoluble, that it was
all a bad dream, the fear (almost ancestral in those of our species)
of being solved—that is, destroyed, killed—affects his state of mind.
In such moments, when we fall prey to the panic of death, as vic-
tims of a solution or of oblivion (a panic created—as the elemen-
tary school manuals explain—through fabrications invented by
humanity, our enemy, in an attempt to exorcise us, such as "No
problem lasts a hundred years" or "Time solves everything" or "No
problem can withstand time," etc.) let us remember that, since the
world began, because of our good fortune and expertise, man has
been incapable of solving any problem; on the contrary, he is ex-
traordinarily well-equipped to create and multiply them as soon as
he prepares to confront any of us.

He closed the book. Crisis. Anguish. Fear of being solved by a
rational human mind. Did such a thing exist? No, those questions didn't concern him in the least. His anguish stemmed
from an unfamiliar source that was very different, perhaps very
distant. His sickness fed on causes unrecognized by the manuals. His sickness. He did not know the source of his sharp, stab-
bing anguish, the feeling that a sword was piercing his breast,
which sometimes hampered his breathing and made him stand
still, on the point of fainting. But—there wasn't the slightest
doubt—his illness had nothing to do with the clinical cases set
forth in the volumes he had been consulting for some time, ever
since his situation had become more and more unbearable.
Fear of being buried alive by human disregard! Fear of senseless, carefree human indifference! Absurd. From childhood,
from his earliest infancy, he had learned that human indifference doesn't exist, much less disregard. The human animal is
resentful. Problems lived on that very thing: on the vices and

spiritual baseness of humanity. On their psychic shabbiness and their inadequate reasoning powers.

Disappointed, he threw down the book. *Possible Disorders in the Adult Problem: Classes, Causes, and Treatment.* It was useless to go on reading. The book seemed to refer to individuals of a different kind, an alien species. Although, really, who was he? What destiny was he fulfilling—or not fulfilling—that was unworthy to appear in the vast bibliography on the wide range of anomalies that could attack his nature as a problem? It wasn't there. His illness was still unknown, unnoticed by others of his kind. Not only was he different from other known problems, he was unique. He knew only too well, however, that his was not a glorious singularity. The golden days of his foolish youth were long, long past, unrecoverable, a time when an irrational hope led him to believe that an honorable existence, devoted to study and the performance of duty, could keep him from the abject end awaiting him as a result of his abominable uniqueness.

He got up with a great effort, feeling nauseous. He could barely hold his head up: it felt like a crushing weight that was growing larger and larger, a strange, dense, floating body attached to his no less strange, dense, floating body. His eyes burned like two balls of fire blurred into a single searing pain. He tried to light a cigarette. His hands shook. It wasn't the sweaty, shivering fear of death that made his whole body tremble that way; it was more like the uncontrollable, ignoble shivering of a wild animal whose entrails are already devoured, when the anguish reaches its legs and slowly travels inside, causing them to jerk in ridiculous spasms more characteristic of a puppet than a creature with a soul.

He managed to place himself in front of the mirror. Now standing in the center of the room, the Problem's entire being was concentrated on an intense desire to see himself. Aware of the meaning of that desire ("It is said," he recited the maxim to himself, "that some Problems are able to see themselves in mirrors before they die"), his eyes rekindled with passion, and tears streamed down his cheeks. He opened his eyes and closed them, not daring to lift his gaze from the floor. He opened them; he closed them. For a few seconds he retained his own image on the dark screen of his tightly closed, tense eyelids. He opened his eyes again and fixed them on the irritated, reddened, swollen eyes that looked at him head on. He stretched one hand toward the ghost with the pale, contorted face, circles under its eyes, tremulous mouth, evident signs of exhaustion and anguish, and an air of stupid surprise that grew stronger and merged with an expression of horror just as his hand touched—not the slim, well-proportioned body attired in light blue, which he saw before him, or the hand that seemingly advanced to join his own, but—the cold, unexpected surface that reflected it.

It was not a cry, but a howl that seemed almost to tear his throat as he rushed at the other person whose body simultaneously hurled itself at his, as if emerging for a battle that took place as he slid, little by little, slowly, down the icy surface, until he fell sobbing to his knees on the floor.

A pleasant sensation began to spread through him and overcome his anxiety: he had to admit that his reflection satisfied him deeply. He liked it. To tell the truth, it filled him with admiration.

How long had it taken him to achieve that more than remarkable image and to fashion a sublime, perfect mask that could hide his true nature? It had required a long, arduous apprenticeship to master the elegant manners, precise, exquisite gestures, subtle words, ambiguous glances, lofty inner thoughts and attitudes that had helped him to distance himself and stand out more and more from the material world. Wrapped in silks and velvets, he had managed to fashion a magnificent look for himself that was totally refined and spiritual. It was impossible for anyone who saw him for the first time to guess what class of problem he belonged to. Hearing him introduce himself as a Metaphysical Problem or as a Problem with Subtle Nuances— an ambition that crossed his existence like a dangerous river in whose waters he would finally drown—no one would ever have dared to doubt his word; for who if not he—a delicate creation, finely wrought of sensitivity and intelligence—constituted, in and of himself, a genuine Subtle Nuance?

But some of his kind did know. As much as he had tried to center conversations—in which he still took part from time to time, always by chance—on subjects about which he had conscientiously acquired knowledge and in which he had been truly brilliant during his years of study and preparation in the hope that his destiny as a Problem might be fulfilled in those noble fields of knowledge (philosophy, literature, oratory, rhetoric, theology, history, methodology, music . . .); and as much as he had pretended absolute ignorance about the psychic and moral nature of human beings and whatever concerned their emotional life, some of his kind knew the tragedy of his life.

But where? Where had his tragedy begun? Perhaps it was already present in his childhood dreams, in the soul of the child he once was, the one they said was a problematical Problem in his school days, the child who had been in school for only a few days when he became the victim of a powerful, extraordinary ambition: to be a Linguistic Problem created by the vulgarization of Latin in the Late Middle Ages, in America, a desire that he replaced—following a serious attack of melancholy after he became convinced, thanks to his preceptors' arduous and exhausting labor, that such a problem was historically, geographically, and culturally impossible—with the conviction that he himself was an Impossible Problem. This romantic ambition, sublimated by the feverish disorders of an illness of tubercular nature, made up an adolescence that was truly unbearable and irritating for those close to him. Yes, perhaps the seeds of his final tragedy were already present in the boy, the student who was so brilliant in all disciplines of an abstract character, whom his classmates still remembered for his ethereal appearance, for the exquisite impression he left in his wake as he passed, and for a few eccentricities, like losing consciousness over and over during the class on Human Problems in which he had to play the role of a Problem among human beings (since this fate awaited most Problems-in-Training, the study of the subject constituted the most complex and important part of their education) or having to leave the classroom, pale and reeling, seized with nausea and violent nervous contractions or shouting uncontrollably as he tried to explain that he felt incapable of occupying the mind of a man or a woman, an ill-conceived, poorly executed landscape, in strident colors and bad taste, embellished — to disguise its fundamental emptiness — with freakish masses of artificial vegetation. If the class focused on the moral, affective, or emotional aspects of the human being, the youngster's weeping and anguish were unassuageable. He despaired when faced with explanations about their bizarre nature— human nature — so weak when it suffered but so implacable and iron-willed when it inflicted suffering; so defenseless before cruelty and injustice, but so firm and strong when it inflicted indiscriminate harm; so petty in action and so prone to repentance. No, young student that he was, he did not want to be a Human Problem; he did not want to cause more harm to the tormented human animal or live in it, the dumping ground of all the detritus of the universe. Some of his age-group remembered how he devoted himself at that time to the painstaking cultivation of his person and his intelligence. His way of dressing, his attire, bearing, and manners were a legend — grotesque for some, charming for others, preposterous for most — whose emergence coincided with the rumor that he was a Problem with problems and with an innocent public confession — obviously imprudent — in which he declared that he had resolved his doubts with respect to his ambition: he was going to be a Problem with Subtle Nuances.

His desolate companions and preceptors observed that, although the Problem was gifted in so many ways, he hadn't managed to accept, or to understand, the essential point on which the future of his existence would depend: he was, and he would be, a Problem. Agrarian? Medical? Mathematical? Domestic? This depended, as did the entire universe, on chance, not on the taste, preference, or aptitudes of the Problem who, like all Problems of his age, had to devote himself, during those years of study, to being trained only as a problem, to learning to be insoluble, confusing, unforgettable, torturous, eternal for the world, for its inhabitants, and for history. "The important thing is to be a problem" was the first lesson of school days. "The same unhappiness can be produced by a religious problem as by a respiratory problem. In the final analysis, its effect always depends on its insolubility."

"What a pity!" sighed his fellow students, when they learned he had succumbed to an ambition. "What a level of confusion he could have attained! He'll never live to be old." Because it was evident that if a Problem felt an ambition then he felt the desire to be a particular way, and the desire to be a particular way involved a problem, a problem different from the Problem who was the problem in himself—an existential incompatibility of which he, the Problem, was conscious and to which he devoted a long, erudite essay that was awarded one of the numerous academic prizes garnered throughout his student life. Because even then he knew, as all fledgling Problems know, that any living being is who he is and what he wishes to be—that is, a double problem, since he is what he doesn't want to be and he isn't what he would like to be. And he also knew that, no matter how insignificant the destructive ability of a problem may seem, it can become limitless if, for example, it operates on a human being, who is, after all, the natural target of every problem. But this destructive ability is fatal for a Problem since he must choose between being the problem he is or being the problem that he has; and plunged into such existential havoc, he must delve deep within himself and finally clarify what problem he is and what problem he has, who he is, what he wants, and why, a process of self-analysis, a bothersome, vexatious investigation in search of self-knowledge, a process of cleansing and clarification of what, as the books say, the human animal calls identity, a process that might lead men to madness but that sweeps Problems to self-solution—to suicide.

Since his youthful work showed that he was aware of the danger inherent in espousing an ambition, why did he insist on pursuing it? Could he have had a premonition? some of his fellow students wondered years later, as they watched the now-adult Problem chatting about barely perceptible subtleties and pretending not to recognize them, the very ones who knew of the great tragedy of his life: that the young Problem (whom they saw leave one day to be introduced—like all Problems that have existed in the world, without regard for origin, race, or color—into God-knows-what mind of what animal in what place in the world, with hopes of passing into history because of the unusual richness of his subtle nuances) had ended up being, plainly and simply, a Sexual Problem.

What would he not have given, throughout the last distressing years, to erase from his painful memory the humiliating recollection of the first moment, after those sweet, theoretical days as a young Apprentice-Problem had gone by, he had suddenly discovered that he was an adult Problem in active service? It was like suddenly waking from an infinite, endless dream. It was like waking into scarlet and blue darkness, dazed and barely able to see or hear anything. First he felt nausea and a growing weakness sweeping over him. Next an unbearable stench suffocated him. He remembered having felt that same disagreeable sensation in the class on . . .

The beginning of a swoon prevented him from crying out; this wasn't a bad dream, a dreadful presentiment. What he never, ever thought could happen to him had happened. He was going to burst, to explode with anger; but he found himself flying through the air. Unexpectedly, someone had given him a kick. He was hurled toward the ceiling of a dimly lit room and landed in the eyes of a man lying in bed, who wrapped him in a furious look and threw him at the eyes of a woman, who from her bed in turn sent him back to the original thrower with a look no less furious. His body ached and his head reeled because he was flying from bed to bed, enveloped in sticky looks that soiled him with hatred, coldness, and vengeful wishes. He couldn't remember from whom—from which criminal mind—

he had emerged. That is, he didn't know whether he belonged to the man or to the woman. Alas, he didn't know what kind of problem he was either, since the two contenders — the man and the woman — both lying down, kept a terrifying silence and had not yet named him.

Later, when some time had gone by, when he tried to reconstruct the moment he met them, when, overcoming his misfortune, he tried to reconstruct, in complete detail, the scene that was to be the first in his existence as a — let's say — Marital Problem, he couldn't remember exactly when disaster had struck and he had lost consciousness. The couple, obsessively fond, as he later had opportunity and time to confirm, of dialectics — that is, devotees of truisms and much given to the absurdity of calling everything by its name — began to talk (or, rather, lie), as he would always hear them talk (or, rather, lie), by resorting to the classic platitudes that usually precede the most wretched falsehoods. So they would say: "Frankly I must tell you," "It sincerely hurts me to admit," "Because the deep affection that joins us is more important than anything." And, inserted between spoken phrases that masked the vilest hatred, they named him out loud. They named him, and they plunged him into eternal ignominy.

He didn't remember, he could never remember, which of the two, he or she, said it first, and it really didn't matter much, since he apparently belonged to them both: not only was he a shared Problem — he, the enemy of all promiscuity — but he was also — he heard it just before he fainted, lost consciousness that would never be the same again — a Sexual Problem.

He came to with aching muscles and ringing ears; bruised, dirty, suit torn to shreds, he passed from female to male mouth with dizzying speed. It was difficult to say which mouth contained more filth, but both were making him disgustingly dirty. "Let's face it!" he heard them shout, referring to him. "Let's admit that it does exist!" they exclaimed, catching him again between their teeth, chewing him up, and passing him from one to the other. The filthier he was, the easier it was for them to recognize him, but, at bottom, neither the man nor the woman wanted him. "I?" "Yes, you." "No, I never. . . ; you . . ."

After a few days, his appearance was pitiful. He displayed various cuts and bruises. He had received so many blows that he felt a single, intense, unbearable pain running through his entire body. Nevertheless, he preferred the physical pain to the other one that plunged him into a melancholy that would end by destroying him if You and I (he never did manage to identify them completely) didn't change their attitude about him. It was really hard to be thrown from lips tight with resentment and end up on others pale with scorn, to go into ears that didn't want to hear, only to go out of others that wanted to deform him, to see himself reduced to a Sexual Problem, something that in another time would not even have had a name; but worst of all was the coldness with which they treated him. He received only looks of hatred and reproach. Neither You nor I ever took any interest in the pitiful, prostrate condition into which he collapsed when they stopped shouting about him. Not one gesture of affection or recognition. They treated him like an outsider, a stranger that had nothing to do with them. After all, wasn't he their problem, even though he was a sexual one? It was discouraging to hear, day after day, that they didn't want him. So why did they insist on keeping him there, admitting him, as they said, if neither of the two accepted him as his or her own? Sometimes he heard them talk about partition. They divided up chairs, children, apartments, money, debts, relatives, friends, books; they even fought about speaking to the concierge, whom neither had addressed for years. But nobody divided him, the Sexual Problem. They blamed him for everything. Every time they named him, they expelled him from their mouths as if to spit him out, and then a barrage of insults and unrepeatable criticism followed him.

What would become of him? He was wiped out, sick, after the discussions that You and I had. Ignored by the inhabitants of the house, he spent sleepless nights, alone, without the much-needed kindness of a friendly word, an affectionate gesture, a grateful thought. When the children saw him, they threw rocks at him; they set cruel, bloody traps for him when he passed. The children hated him. You and I, a modern couple, considered it indispensable to announce the appearance of the Sexual Problem in their home, and, taking advantage of a family picnic, they decided to discuss him in the presence of those tender little ears and inform them about real life and about the true reasons for the perpetual state of domestic war. From then on, the children hated him.

With makeup, cosmetics, suits of impeccable cut, and a haughty expression, he disguised his wretched condition as a Sexual Problem, as a sad — a sadder and sadder — Sexual Problem. Very infrequently, a chance meeting with former classmates offered him the opportunity to converse about subjects from bygone days — a very questionable version of some Homeric poetry or a Debussy piece — and he felt a lump in his throat. If You or I could see him, they would understand how valuable, deep down, their Sexual Problem was, endowed with knowledge and talents that they didn't even suspect. During such melancholy conversations, he learned of the various positions filled by his former companions: one had become a social problem, a really serious social problem; another had gotten to be a heraldic problem that world specialists in the field would not manage to untangle for centuries; little so-and-so had revolutionized the field of metaphysics with a question that set Saint Thomas at odds with Aristotle forever and paired him with Marx; little what's-his-name . . .

Why did he have to be the one? What would he not give to be another kind of problem, even a political one? He returned home, strolled through the house, walked through the library, stroked the spines of the books. Although he had already read all of the books that You and I owned, at times he tried to reread one. He was so weak, however, that the volume would fall from his hands, which lacked the strength to hold it; the letters crowded together in a dark, confused smudge when he tried to stare at them with eyes that clouded over after a few seconds. He was obliged to sit down or to lean on the back of the chair, over-come by a mild dizzy spell that stupefied him. If he tried again, he managed to read a few lines, but their meaning was incom-patible with what he had read a moment before.

This inability to concentrate on the reading sank him into a state closer to melancholy than to desperation. At times he imagined what would happen if, when he was in the library, You and I would come in ready to begin one of their timeworn "considerations of our relationship," as they would say, that is, a long, incoherent, and boring discussion about him; what would happen, wondered the Problem, if he interrupted them with an open book in his hands and recited . . . Did they like poetry? He admitted his ignorance of what kind of pleasures You and I en-joyed in their leisure. Although, on reflection, he reached the conclusion that they had no pleasures at all. Before, it seemed, they often went to the movies. But since he, the Problem, had arrived, they stayed home to discuss him. How he would have preferred for them to take him to the movies! Because the worst of it was not that he was a Sexual Problem or even a shared Problem; it wasn't their lack of consideration, or the fatigue and disgust of leaping from mouth to mouth, or the boredom. The worst thing, for him, was that You and I had other Problems.

When You and I began their usual talk about their Sexual Problem, a swarm of Problems immediately appeared, ready for a fierce struggle. It was not You and I they were against; they were against him, against the Sexual Problem, an obstacle that hindered their own work. You and I had an Economic Problem, a Problem of the Children, a Problem of Living Together, a Problem of Boredom, a Problem of Agreement, a Problem of Loneliness, a Problem of Indifference, a Problem of Incom-patibility of Character, a Problem of Independence . . . All of them, conspiring together, attacked the newcomer—the Sexual Problem—claiming their seniority, their seriousness, and their leading role in the matter of You and I's affairs. A role, a senior-ity, and a seriousness they were unwilling to renounce in favor of the Sexual Problem, an intruder, a modern, newfangled, inexperienced Problem that hindered them from carrying out their work.

The Problem of Conscience that You and I harbored was the one who saved him from the frying pan only to throw him into the fire when he called for duty and goodwill, as is usual with all Problems of Conscience. The unwary Sexual Problem fell into every trap set by the Problem of Conscience during his cunning interrogations disguised as a friendly dialogue. Yes, confessed the Sexual Problem, he knew that You and I had a friend, Margarita, whom the Problem of Conscience called "the other woman." He could provide little information about the young woman, because when I, accompanied by the Sexual Problem, went to Margarita's house, he—the Sexual Problem—was barely mentioned. They put out the light as if he didn't exist; he relaxed and took advantage of the time to sleep. They were the most peaceful hours of his hard days, those and the ones that You spent at Manolo's house. Didn't the Problem of Conscience know who Manolo was? Did he only suspect his existence?

Once the suspicion became certainty, the Problem of Conscience exploded. His nature didn't admit deception, and even beyond the question of solidarity with a fellow problem was the need to safeguard his own tranquillity, his honor, and his dignity. Expressed brutally, the truth might kill the Sexual Problem, but, unspoken, silenced, it would kill the Problem of Conscience, who didn't hesitate to declare it: "You don't exist. You're a problem invented by them. You and I do have a sexual problem, but it is called Margarita and Manolo."

"At last, *La cuestión fundamental*," thought the Sexual Problem before closing his eyes, remembering a quotation by an author he had read in his days as a scholarly problem. He believed that the pain rending his chest and the white cloud gradually descending on his mind was death.

But no, the pain rending his chest was not death, and when the Sexual Problem began to recover from a long period of unconsciousness, it was spring and he longed to be in the sun, by the window, dozing a little, meditating a little, reminiscing a little. Sunken in this mental semi-emptiness, which at another time he would have repudiated but which was pleasurable now, his thoughts hurt less. The extraordinary facility of human beings for practicing forgetfulness surprised the Problem. Because after Margarita and Manolo came Rafael and Luisa, Carlos and Lola, Pedro and Mercedes, Jacinto and Nieves. Years later, he was to admit that in spite of everything the life that You, I, and he shared at that time was the best period of his existence. Gradually, the couple's other Problems stopped bursting into the household and pursuing him, the Sexual Problem, to reproach him with his falseness. Some, like the Problem of Living Together, the Problem of Incompatibility of Character, the Problem of Jealousy . . . moved to Margarita's house when I went there and to Manolo's house with You. And the rest of the couple's Problems barely had the strength to attempt any violent action against him, being, as indeed they were, completely demoralized; since You and I almost never mentioned them or fought because of them, they stopped worrying about them, and what are problems if no one worries about them?

On the other hand, the false Sexual Problem felt quite protected, if not exactly happy. You and I saw each other seldom, but when the two met alone, it was to speak about him; and although, as the Problem of Conscience had told him, he didn't exist, what did he care since he, the false Problem, was the couple's favorite subject? Besides, he was their only link. If he left them, what would become of them? He had grown fond of them. Yes, in a certain way, he loved them. He would remain with them forever. He would see them grow old together: You and I, stooped, with gray hair, wrinkled skin, and faded eyes, would continue talking about him during their long, slow walks in the sun or sitting on a park bench . . .

The Sexual Problem looked at himself in the mirror. He was determined to find out. Did he or didn't he exist? In any case, the end would be the same. He wanted to stop existing or stop not existing. He knew: Problems can see themselves in mirrors before they die.

Tears ran down his cheeks. You and I and the memories they had shared crossed his mind. How foolish to have grown fond of them. What he had learned in school was true: "Human beings never solve any problem." But they replace them, he thought. They replace them quickly. A new Manolo appeared, or a new Margarita, even more Manolo-like or more Margarita-like than the previous ones, and again, the disastrous practice of confession, with *honestly* and *frankly* covering up hatred, vengeance, and lies. Both shouted it. You and I, together, a dev-ilish gleam in their eyes, with voices that seemed shot out of a deadly weapon instead of coming from mere human throats: no, he, the Sexual Problem, didn't exist, he had never existed, the truth was . . .

That he had never existed, repeated the Problem to himself in front of the mirror; and the other one, facing him, dressed in light blue, repeated that it was true, he had never existed. Im-possible, he murmured, together with the one in the mirror. It was impossible not to exist. He lived. Whether false or true, he did live; they said it in unison, wide-open eyes staring into wide-open eyes. False or true, what did it matter? The impor-tant thing was that he did indeed live; he existed. The proof was there, in the mirror. False or true. It was only a question of subtle nuances . . . A question of subtle nuances. The Problem standing in front of the mirror and the Problem reflected in the mirror hit their heads against the smooth surface. Had he been a Problem with Subtle Nuances during that dreadful, lengthy period when he thought he was a false Sexual Problem? Had he been what he had wanted to be without knowing it? Who, who was he really? He would find out, even if it cost him his life. Yes, he was going to die, to disappear. He himself would figure him-self out, he himself would identify himself. Self-solution was death. But he would find out, he would find out by entering the mirror—which is what the suicidal Problem finally did.

Exactly a third of the Problem was left to enter, to disappear in the mirror in search of himself, when You and I, in a new confrontation that began as if it would be the very last one and ended inconclusively, reaffirmed his existence. And the final third of the Problem's body stayed outside the mirror . . . It stayed . . . It stayed.

From that day on, a piece of Problem has been walking the earth. It is said that because of the mishap he suffered in front of a mirror he is an incoherent, bothersome Problem who cries easily, becomes irritated for no reason, and never knows what he really wants. Sometimes he thinks he is a Sexual Problem, at other times, a false Sexual Problem; some days he declares that he is a Problem with Subtle Nuances. He hates for people to recognize him on the street, to ask for his autograph; he loathes seeing himself in newspapers and on television. Sometimes he manages to escape from the universities and schools where he is acclaimed and studied as the problem of the century. Then it is not unusual to find him in a dark corner of a filthy bar, drinking too much and telling the story of his life to anyone willing to listen.

THE DEAD

What she dreads especially about the large dinner parties she gives at home is the beginning. Or even more, perhaps, the end. Because the beginning of the party goes faster than the end. If people arrive on time, the first moments of the gathering pass more quickly than the last ones, slipping by with numbing speed. And between the first drink, which she downs hastily during the last-minute preparations in an effort to replace the weariness she experiences at the thought of greeting friends with the strength it takes to welcome them cordially, and the unavoidable duty—preceded by the doorbell's ring—of welcoming the first arrivals, the beginning of the party usually turns out to be more bearable than she had feared. And of course, there is always someone who arrives right on time. Breathing deeply, she finally relaxes, giving in to a sudden calm. Besides, the preliminary drinks always manage to produce the desired mood change. That's doubtless why everyone seeks out her company during the opening moments of her parties, when she is "really charming," "delightful," and "always so witty and jolly." In fact, she is surprised to hear herself laughing, her laughter not forced because she wants to create a certain congenial atmosphere among the guests but, rather, unforced because she realizes that she is utterly gracious, floating in the sudden state of well-being that seems such a natural quality to her now, in contrast with the irritable, unpleasant mood of the last hours.

When she woke up in the morning with the upsetting idea of the party scheduled for that evening and the crushing certainty of her inability to endure the beginning of the gathering, why hadn't she managed to convince herself that her morning inertia invariably disappears with the first drinks and the first guests? Then she feels so at ease, as if she is gliding among the smooth stalks of the weird plant life that a room full of friends eventually resembles.

Yes, now she realizes she is engulfed in a kind of delicious effervescence, like sparkling water. She feels herself emerge triumphantly from a champagne-like bubbling through which the vision of the world makes an agreeable spectacle, a scene in which she isn't displeased to appear, even as an active participant. Yes, now she looks at the living room and the terrace that leads to the garden as if they were a stage on which it will be easy for her to play a limited role, somewhat more showy and animated than a simple extra's part, the insignificant walk-on's part, to which she had resigned herself under the influence of the relentless depression she had suffered since waking. She also imagines, however, that the simple wandering about called for by her minor role as hostess is connected with both the enormous effort to pull it off and a certain fear . . . Yes, now as she hears the complimentary remarks of Enrique Loreto, young and embarrassed, the first guest to arrive, about the arrangements of hydrangeas and peonies scattered around the room, she feels light and bubbly in the midst of the stage set that she has so feared, and she smiles condescendingly at herself as she remembers the feeling, a mixture of panic and reluctance, that overcame her this morning when, no sooner had she opened her eyes, a thought forced itself imperiously into her consciousness and cut her sleep off for good: "Tonight is the anniversary party."

On the other hand, as she now looks at herself in the mirror out of the corner of her eye, as she looks for the image of her face among the reflected bouquets of flowers, she sees herself laugh, perhaps exaggeratedly. She wonders why she should laugh so much when she answers the embarrassed and disconcerted Loreto's timid question: "Has Miguel arrived yet?" Her remark by way of a reply is supposed to be lighthearted but still can't help sounding trite: "He has just arrived and is getting ready. You know how conceited poets are. Or could you be an exception?" As she looks at herself in the mirror, sees herself laugh, and admits she is satisfied, agreeably satisfied with the image of her thirty-odd years, a thought, the opposite of the one she had this morning, tickles her consciousness: she is happy, happy, and feels like shouting. Shouting, shouting until she is hoarse and panting, her body exhausted, with every sensation she is capable of feeling worn away.

When she wakes up in the morning with the crushing certainty that she will be unable to endure the beginning of a party or of any type of gathering no matter how small and that she will be incapable of carrying out any activity planned the day before, why can't she remember that in the end, when the moment arrives, she always accomplishes what she has set herself to do? In the morning when she wakes up, why doesn't she repeat to herself over and over that when the moment comes, in the end, she always does what her lethargic mind believes is going to take a heroic, titanic effort and is no more difficult than keeping an appointment with a friend, going to the theater or the hairdresser, going out shopping, making the necessary arrangements with Alicia so that everything at home will follow the rhythm set by the strictest daily routine and so that nothing, nothing will deviate from its normal pattern, so that in the course of the day, there are no jarring incidents to alter the fixed routine and allow the outside world to see the profound disconnection that stifles and chokes her as soon as she takes her eyes off the most immediate reality and turns them inward to the center of her being?

But no, when she wakes up in the mornings, no matter how normal the events of the new day seemed the night before when she was planning them, there is no way to convince herself that they will turn out to be less overwhelming than she foresees at that moment. Feeling ill, she wakes up late—later, when she looks at her clock, than what she decides would have been prudent in order to have enough time to arrange the day's chores without exhausting herself. The weariness that prevents her from getting up is real sickness, she tells herself. The early morning glare, which the blinds and drawn curtains filter without blocking out completely, bursts violently into the bedroom; it jumps from the window onto the bed and at her face, like brilliant snakes ready to attack her with their deadly bite, the sign of a new day ahead. After the slithering, blinding flashes implacably bite her eyelids again, they lose their virulence and gradually stop striking her half-closed eyes with tongues of light that follow one after another from her retina to her brain, like stunning flashes of a powerful spotlight, then dissolve into indistinct light that fills the bedroom. She turns over in bed or covers her head with the fold of the sheet, trying to find enough darkness to create an illusion of night that will deny the morning already glimpsed, the hour indicated by the clock, the breakfast ready by the bed.

Go back to sleep. For years, that has been the first wish of the day. Go back to sleep. Sometimes she manages it aided by the stupor typical of waking from a drugged sleep with a hangover. Although frequently that same sluggishness, the feeling of physical and mental torpor, turns into an apprehensive uneasiness that forces her to get out of bed. But to do what? She doesn't know. Or she does. There are a thousand things to do, a thousand places to go, a thousand people to see. Obligations, almost all of them, she tells herself. And she sees herself doing, seeing, going. She doesn't want to look at the series of pictures formed in her mind, in which she sees herself doing what she planned the day before: pictures of herself walking along such-and-such a street on the way to such-and-such a shop, pictures of herself buying a certain fruit or certain flowers, pictures of herself trying on a dress or trying out a hairdo, pictures of herself deciding not to take a certain street, to enter a certain shop, to buy certain flowers, to go to meet a certain person with whom she has made a date. She sees herself putting down a certain record half-pulled out of its jacket, a certain book half-read . . . And, utterly exhausted, one by one she discards the pictures of herself going through the day. Merely imagining herself in action drains her. She decides to think about something else. To think about something for which she doesn't have to go outside or fix herself up. To think about something, about someone, not herself. Not to see herself, not to think about herself. The children.

No, not that either. Not the children. It is absolutely, inviolably forbidden to think about the children, to allow any child-related reference into a mind like hers, which struggles in a fog when she wakes. This is an unbreakable rule to prevent the en-circling nets of her excruciating morning thoughts from trap-ping the children's figures and swallowing them in their dizzy-ing, bottomless vortex. No, not the children. It is imperative not to think. Not to see herself, not to think about herself. But the children: no, not that either. It is imperative to stop, to halt the series of pictures of herself, the stream of pictures that upset her as much when they depict her starting any action as when they reproduce her wandering through the house, dragging herself wearily from an easy chair and a half-read newspaper to a sofa and a half-opened letter; from a mirror that reflects her with half-combed hair to a half-filled bathtub; from a half-dialed telephone to a half-arranged bouquet of daisies. Not to see her-self, not to think about herself. But the children: no. Not that ei-ther. She has a sudden attack of severe breathlessness if the smiling faces of the children or their bodies frozen in a certain familiar posture manage to erupt into her thoughts, to knock down the leaden walls of her mind without warning. A lead box—that's how she pictures the mind that contains her train of thoughts: a lead box filled with nothing but lead. Real panic overcomes her, and she feels a clammy chill when a feature, a child's voice surreptitiously manages to filter into that opaque, dense space that weighs her down in the very core of her being. It is fear and desolation. Because if she doesn't manage to drive away the sudden vision of the children, what at first is only the fleeting snapshot of an expression turns into a concrete, de-tailed picture in her mind as it persists. And one or both of the children talk to her, they tell her stories, and in that ordinary daily scene, a real scene that is then reproduced on the dis-jointed, alarming film whose disconnected frames assail her when she wakes up, they say something to her that she is mak-ing an effort to understand. Do they notice it? Do they notice the exhausting effort with which she sometimes tries to understand the meaning of a simple phrase, an ordinary, inane question? When she takes one of their small heads between her hands and squeezes it with controlled force, the apparent caress is really an attempt to discover — by touch — an idea, the meaning of something that has been explained out loud and has reached her ears but not her faculty of understanding. At that point, do the children's eyes, as they look at her eagerly for a reply, read in her eyes total emptiness, see her plunged into total emptiness by the overwhelming discovery that the words uttered by the young mouths are totally unconnected? Her fingers press those soft, fresh lips that, despite the obstacle of their mother's frantic contact, do not stop moving, opening and closing on the pronunciation of words that have for her only isolated, disjointed meanings; but the connections that do take place between sound and concept are short-lived because they get lost; they fall into oblivion as soon as she starts the mechanical operation of trying to group them into a complete sentence. And then, in the face of an impossible reciprocation on her part, and despite her indifference to the children's plans, she offers a hug, or even a playful remark or expression that can turn the situation in another direction and even end it there. It is a matter of momentarily suspending conversation with the children, of silencing them, of interrupting their chatter, of hushing the young voices that bewilder her and take her unaware like an air raid carried out in the name of some alien, unfathomable cause before which she can only choose between two positions: either give up and allow herself to be completely overpowered, letting them fire all the salvos of their absurd celebration without resisting or answering in kind; or deflect the attack toward other targets — Alicia, if she is available, or Miguel, if he is at home, or the false urgency of wholly unnecessary tasks. Send them away, direct them toward other victims, toward other opponents more resistant than she, as if it were a matter of shaking off the attack of a bothersome but insignificant enemy who inspires only weariness and indifference. Oh no, when she wakes up, she can't bear to think about the children. She feels a lump in her throat and she inhales convulsively for endless moments before bursting into tears that continue to sting her eyelids until half the day has gone by. The children. If they were home now . . . Yes, she will pay more attention to them; when they come back from school she will plan something with them. A trip downtown or a game; they love her to take part in their games. Yes, she wants to see them, to touch them, to squeeze them hard, almost until she hears them shriek as they do—their three bodies rolling on the floor or on the bed—during their fierce make-believe fights, pretending to be wild animals. Yes, she wants to see them, to be with them now. For that, in order to be in suitable physical condition, she must stop crying, avoid the headache that usually follows the tears and the tension of those absurdly distressing awakenings. She is impatient: how many hours are left before the children come home from school? Maybe she will go and pick them up. But what to do until midafternoon? There are a thousand things to do. The party! Again the feeling of inertia, of exhaustion that prevents her from leaving the bed and the bedroom once and for all, thrusts upon her, with the force of utter certainty, the conviction that she is sick.

But now, at the party, she feels good, wonderfully good. At last all the guests have arrived, or almost all. Some fifty guests whom she has been greeting with an enthusiasm that has replaced her inertia, thanks to Miguel, who—fortunately, she thinks—has appeared in the living room, impeccable in his light-colored suit. Even after years, she is aware of his almost subtle elegance. His self-possessed manner isn't contagious, but at least it relieves her of having to pretend she is calm, so now she can speak and walk around without having to hide completely the nervousness that a drawn-out succession of hugs, kisses, and festive greetings always makes her feel. Most of all, congratulations. Because today the congratulations follow one another and are about to agitate the emotional undercurrent just calmed by the first drinks.

The repeated congratulations offered by the guests who have

been arriving at the anniversary party seem to form a circle around her, like the shapeless members of an army that is invisible but ready for a surprise attack. She knows the circle is undefined and, for the moment, wide but able to close in on her at any second. But not yet, she thinks with the certainty that she is untouchable as long as she stays in the center of the fluctuating space into which an agitated but euphoric happiness has deposited her. While she remains buoyantly in this glassed-in, tingly shelter that seems to enclose her, the congratulations aimed at her will not reach their target. She is floating, encased in a bubble, and they can't reach her. She allows the congratulations to move around the room, to cross the room crowded with people and laughter, to rise into the air like paper streamers that her now powerful will preordains to disintegrate after a weak, colorful flight. A magic ball transports and isolates her within its luminous, transparent walls, against which the excuse for so much well-wishing smashes.

She doesn't feel a part of that marriage for which the fifteenth anniversary party is being held, or affected—as apparently some voices that reach her from very far away, she believes, assume she is—by Miguel's new book of poems, whose publication is also being celebrated today. "If I were you, I would feel so proud," whispers Mónica Zumoi in her ear as she puts her arms around her but doesn't quite give her a hug, just as her lips don't quite manage the expected kiss on the cheek; those lips are thin, she thinks—too thin—and parted in a tense smile, an edgy smile she doesn't see but imagines, while at her ear she hears the hesitant words of recrimination disguised as flattery: "If I were you, I would feel so proud." And when Mónica's tanned face pulls away from hers and their arms, which have hardly brushed in the sham of an embrace, separate, it seems that, rather than draw back a few inches to stand in front of Mónica, she moves away, moves away toward the back of the room, places herself at the other end of the room near the terrace leading to the garden, from where Mónica's blue eyes continue staring at her, a forced smile on her too-thin lips.

Blonds with light-colored eyes and overthin lips have always made her wary. And given her a chilly feeling: that false, sudden chill that embarrassment produces in her. And especially Mónica Zumoi. The enveloping quality of her rather mellow voice is negated by the icy edge of her gaze, and what she means to say, whatever it may be, is contradicted by precarious lips that expose the wet pink gum line as they open too wide in a catlike grin. To believe in Mónica's words is an act of will for her. Suspicion or jealousy, Miguel would scoff. But usually she has the feeling that a famished sincerity has devoured small mouths because they are never completely exposed. She is afraid to see the wiry mechanism of Mónica's steely sensibility showing through behind those dull, light-colored eyes.

Nevertheless, as she looks at Mónica now, she admits that not only is she beautiful in her black dress but also openly affectionate. The golden skin of her arms and bare shoulders—healthy but slim supports of an abundant mane of blond hair—exudes a certain tenderness, a disturbing, extremely pleasant warmth to which a tickling sensation in her own body responds with pleasure. She likes to feel this kind of physical affection toward someone from whom, as is the case with Mónica, she is ordinarily separated by an invisible wire fence not made of demonstrable ill will but of uneasy, hypothetical incompatibilities. What a delightful sensation of well-being to feel how that mesh of barbed prejudices first gradually loses its obstructive power and then ends up totally obliterated because no one hears its alarm signals. It is wonderful, she thinks, to feel how the ice of aversion between two people melts and is replaced by an intense, caressing warmth that slowly spreads between them in spite of the yards that separate them—as they do her and Mónica—a powerful warmth like the burning swell that rises from the belly to the face when one takes the first sips from a glass of wine.

But no, she thinks, as she hears her own voice in cheerful conversation with someone or other, those yards of distance between them are nonexistent. It isn't possible for Mónica to be where she thinks she sees her—at the other end of the room—

because, standing between them, Alberto Zumoi puts his arms around their shoulders, pulling them toward each other until their heads bump, and addresses his remark to them: "Fifteen years of marriage! That's some record! And to a poet, which is like saying to a madman!"

"But a brilliant madman," adds someone she pretends not to recognize and places, because of his barely used black tuxedo and the overdone, affected cut of his gray hair, in the vague memory of a vague dinner party with some bankers.

"A madman with a muse, my friend!" she hears Alberto go on insistently. "A madman with an exceptional muse. That is the only difference between a simple madman and a brilliant poet: the brilliant poet has muses and a publisher like me; on the other hand, the poor madman has at best only nurses who take away his inspiration with cold showers and a doctor who isn't at all like me and who does just the opposite of what I do — instead of giving money, he just gives advice!"

As he bursts out laughing, Alberto Zumoi's jerky movement separates her slightly from Mónica, and once again she sees Mónica far away, at a distance she knows is nonexistent.

She knows that distance, those false distances perceived by her senses when euphoria brushes them; her senses are like stringed instruments plucked by a magical hand, from which euphoria draws registers and sensorial nuances far beyond their real possibilities. So Mónica is not at the other end of the room. She herself is the one there, at the other end of the room, and at the same time at this end, next to the two Zumois. She is — she feels that she is — everywhere. At this very moment, without taking a step, she is with young, embarrassed Enrique Loreto as they make the rounds of various groups of friends, preferentially organized, as was to be expected, around or near — as near as possible — Jasmina and Devora Poe, the leading ladies in Miguel's latest play; and she is accompanying Miguel, also at this very moment and also without taking a step, making the difficult initial contact with a critic who has protected himself behind a wall of ill-concealed discomfort — because he is meeting at this party more of the creative sensibilities wounded by his pen than he would have wished — and behind Matilda's exultant sympathy.

She mustn't disregard Matilda Orozco, left alone in some out-of-the-way, neglected corner; she mustn't allow her venerable presence to be forgotten, as usually happens at most of the gatherings that exceed more than half a dozen people. At first, all the guests there seem to compete for her company and for their turn to pay their deep, universal, and unquestionably genuine respect; but as the party progresses, they apparently prefer to exchange Matilda's outgoing but demanding benevolence, her conversation, which is rich and stimulating but seamlessly inaccessible to stupidity, for lighter and more comfortable substitutes.

Without moving (oh! it's the scent of the narcissus that is the medium that transports and spreads her throughout the space it fills!), she follows the waiters' zigzagging path through the guests and sees to it that they all have everything they need. She will go, she must go meet Miguel and his critics; for young Loreto, she will facilitate easy conversation with people whom for the most part he doesn't know; she will supply Matilda with conversationalists at her demanding level; she will manage to establish bonds of congeniality and lightheartedness that will cancel out the lack of common interests, differences of criteria, and manifold dissimilarities among the various groups of friends whose activities take place in such far-flung areas as theater, literature, banking, politics, academic life, and the world of entertainment.

Now she remembers how Miguel and Mónica Zumoi enjoyed themselves the night they prepared the guest list together. From the study on the floor above, Mónica's excited voice and Miguel's deep, lazy laughter reached her room, reached her bed, at dawn. "A selection of people thoughtfully and purposely drawn up so no one gets on with anyone else. It will be an unforgettable party!" they explained to her the next day. "All you have to do is let them skin each other alive and not worry as they drop dead of boredom in the corners, one by one."

She isn't worried, of course; nor will she worry, she tells herself. She knows perfectly well that no one skins anyone else completely, nor is it so serious to get bored. The list of names made up by Miguel and Mónica—similar, moreover, to the lists for the usual parties—has at no time inspired worry or fear of possible embarrassing situations, just inertia. The same inertia as always, the inertia aroused by any succession of names and faces that adds up to more than four or five. She is not the one upset by worry or fear; it is Miguel, who, she knows and has verified only a few hours ago, once the moments of carefree delight in Mónica's company or in the company of anyone who would be his ally in similarly amusing situations have passed, falls into doubt and obsessive vacillation between the advisability of facing events as they have been designed and the possibility of changing the plans completely at the last minute.

Inertia is her only enemy. Once the battle against paralyzing sluggishness is over, she cares little about the kind of scene that awaits her because she is basically indifferent to the figures in it; and in the last analysis, the supposed pleasure or anguish that stems from her fleeting relationship with these figures always depends on the place from which she observes them. On the other hand, Miguel seems to despise any panoramic scene, especially in the presence of Mónica or any person or persons who witness his observation; but in reality, each and every one of the figures that contribute to the scene interests him deeply and almost painfully. It is a graduated interest that oscillates between intensity, if it arises and remains as a means of finally possessing the object in question, and total indifference, if he guesses that possession is impossible. That is why, she thinks, Miguel is unable to enjoy scenes that don't concern him. That is why she sees him now, going from one guest to another, taking it on himself to be attentive and not turn his back on anyone, worried and repressing his unfulfillable desire to attend simultaneously to everyone there, to attend to them with the amiability, wit, and affection that irresistibly drive him. He needs to captivate everyone, because if even one of the guests doesn't speak to him about his latest book or his latest play, the party will be a disaster for him. It doesn't matter if the object of his seduction is Matilda's brilliant mind, Julio Rotellar's exceptional talent, Rita Melo's beauty, or the coarse mediocrity of Masanés the banker, with whom, at this moment, Miguel is keeping up a lively conversation and above whose bald head he restlessly watches her. When their glances meet, he winks and smiles. He smiles openly, but not without some nervousness, one hand in his pants pocket and his slim torso leaning slightly forward, as if he were going to break in two. He waits for her to smile back so he can redirect the expectant glance he is giving her. She knows that he is waiting for an affirmative answer from her eyes or a movement of her lips in answer to the question that the room full of people raises for him. In the tense arch of his virile eyebrows and in the teeth clenched on the mouthpiece of his pipe, she grasps his urgent need to receive a reassuring gesture equivalent to a general approval: everything is perfect; no, there are not too many people, and besides, they are very well chosen.

And she reassures him with a smile and an affirmative movement of her head. From the bubbly space in which she is floating, she thinks Miguel's efforts to be a good host are childish. From her observation point, it feels wonderful to let herself go from one guest to another simply because she wishes to do so, to look at them all at the same time and to feel the fiber of their souls, suddenly accessible thanks to the prodigious tactile ability of her thought. Like a knife, she plunges into everyone there and passes through them, and at the same time, she is outside them, watching them. Yes, she will go, of course she will go, to pay her respects to old Cabral. She will do it, of course. It isn't the same thing to think it as to do it, she reproaches herself. It isn't the same thing to think that she will go up to Devora Poe and tell her how charmed she was by her performance in Miguel's latest play and that Devora couldn't possibly know how important it was for him to work with her, as it is to pick up a drink, light a cigarette, and make her way toward the actress. No, she tells herself, it isn't the same thing to think it as to do it, although while she thinks it, she may feel she is doing it, and she may even see Devora's large sunflower-yellow eyes narrow as they smile at her and hear her sincere regrets at being forced to leave Devora's charming company for a moment to show the garden to the Dondis. Now she remembers that they want to see the magnolia tree. As soon as she catches them standing near the terrace, she will cross the room and go with them out into the garden. Yes, and she will breathe in the exhilarating scent of the magnolias! In fact, she believes she is smelling them from here. She smiles. At no one. At a fresh glass of champagne drained almost in a single swallow to increase the intensity of the fantastic sensorial ecstasy that allows her to inhale the coolness of the magnolias as if she really were close to them in the distant garden. She also believes that the sweet smell of the wisteria clinging to the roof of her mouth, to her own skin, and to the skin of the people around her is real. Holding her breath, eyes half-closed, slowly moving her tongue inside her mouth, she savors the luminous skin on bare arms and shoulders, the dark, secret skin on the napes of tanned necks. She tries to retain the honeyed wisteria-taste that her tongue's slow, imaginary stroll extracts from languid hands, resting passively on others' shoulders; from tense, lean hands, busy with drinks and cigarettes; from throats encased in silk and in shirt collars with ties; from soft throats, open to the possibility of contact; from bodies relaxed in the rhythm of the conversation.

She looks at those bodies. Indistinctly discernible among the bluish splotches of the hydrangeas and the red of the peonies, they drink, they chat, they make casual gestures. Until tonight, she never liked the decor of the living room, imposed by Marco, the set-designer for Miguel's plays. "Overwhelming? What could be simpler than an empty space between two facing walls that have been totally covered with mirrors?" An enormous rectangle formed on its short sides by two walls of glass—one of which indicates the entrance to the living room and the other, the exit to the garden—and on the long sides by mirrors. Two mirror-walls she has never liked. But now, allowing herself to see the flowers reflected in duplicate, she is charmed, and she admits—she has wasted almost the entire day in doubt—that it was a good idea to alternate the blue of the hydrangeas and the red of the peonies with the yellow narcissus and the white acacia flowers from the garden. Yes, the scent of narcissus is the medium that transports and conveys her through space! The scent carries her and brings her closer to the faces reflected in the mirrors on both sides of the room. As she inhales it deeply, it penetrates her chest and loosens the tangled net that all day long has been tugging at the core of her being, almost turning her breathing into labored panting. But now the scent of the narcissus makes its way into her mouth, her throat, pulling in the warmth of the voices that seem to emerge like soothing, sweet organ music around her. As she—and what she is—slowly exhales the scent, she follows it. What? she thinks, what is she?—a collection of tiny feelings, like diminutive brilliant points that twinkle and show up against a dark background, gathered into a single feeling capable of rising above the body where it is produced, like an electric current that might burst into sparks and electrify the air around the edges of the elements that generate it. She, whatever she may be, continues on, escapes from her body with the scented exhalation of what becomes a trail, a thin wake, which crosses the room until it finally strikes the polished, cool, almost cold surfaces of the mirrors, like a bird exhausted but ecstatically overwhelmed in its own weariness. Oh, to fly swiftly over the groups of guests, impelled by the fragrance of narcissus until she is fused to the mirrors, submerged in a bath of light and coolness. Fused to the mirror. Whoever may be chatting on the sofa means nothing to a person who must ascend to fulfill her desire: to hold out her arms and press her body—her whole body—against the mirror; to rub against the surface with all her strength in order to enter it and become an image. Simply be an image—not the exterior body that projects it—simply be an image inside the icy surface and watch the party from there. Because it is hot, she thinks. The heat begins to be felt; it rises from the bottom of the glasses and from conversations that seem disconnected now to her; it envelops her in a sickening, reddish mist, and clouds her eyes.

She doesn't move forward. The stroll among the groups of friends, which has been magical until now, loses its momentum. The fantastic thrust that was transporting her weakens little by little, and she fears it will not manage to propel her to the mirror. Not even to the terrace. The faces, smiling as soon as they see her looking at them—the made-up faces, the tanned faces, the necks and more or less bejeweled décolletages, the shoulders in dark- or light-colored jackets that mill around her now—are the same: they don't vary, they don't follow one another in different forms as they did when she passed them only a few seconds ago in an invisible stroll that made her light and free.

She blinks in an effort to recover the tingly vision of the halo of lights that, a few minutes ago—hardly any time—enveloped the guests and sparked as they brushed against one another. It has gone out in this reddish semidarkness made up of tobacco smoke and too many peonies. It was like a glowing, meteoric fluttering through the trees of a thick, illuminated forest, a fluttering whose wild path she followed riding on a beam of ghostly light. And now she feels riveted to the floor; a leaden heaviness overcomes her and holds her motionless, imprisoned in the cramped space created by dense, slimy vegetation. She wants to flee from this dank gloom, to rise above the menacing tree trunks that advance and close around her in a circle that will eventually squeeze and choke her. To recover the thrust of the flight so she can crash into the cool polish of the mirrors; she thinks they are hideous after all, and they give the room and its walk-on actors an unpleasant underwater appearance. In the grotesque mirror-walls, the room is an aquarium that contains them all. She closes her eyes for a moment to keep her balance, which she almost loses when she finds Marga's undulating figure turning into a fish. Or maybe it's not a metamorphosis? she wonders. To tell the truth, Marga's unblinking eyes, round as if in perpetual surprise, and her chalky complexion with its bluish, pearly transparency betray in the ichthyological display into which the evening light has turned the sparkling walls of the living room an undoubtedly fishlike nature. Yes, if she opens her eyes and looks toward the mirrors, she feels submerged in an aquarium in whose foul, reddish waters the freakish shapes of the guests in their evening clothes sway as they try frantically to breathe among the corpses of the hydrangeas; but if she closes her eyes, the oppressive crowd around her turns back into its woody state, and now menacing plants are what prevent her from moving. Alberto Zumoi's rough, elongated arms sprout from a sinewy, coarse trunk and encircle her shoulders like sinister branches; the publisher's loud guffaws emerge from a bushy treetop as he laughs at his own silly witticisms about the fifteenth anniversary of some marriage or other that she knows nothing about.

Laugh, say something. She can't. She notices her dry throat, her empty glass. The only waiter capable of helping her — she decides after calculating that he is the nearest — is in an opening, the only opening visible along her impossible route and too far away from the path she thinks she should begin now, right now, to follow. Yes, she must move, she must reach the small opening left by the groups of guests near the terrace. She must move quickly toward the spot without allowing time for the waiter to disappear, without waiting to be overtaken by Gustavo and by Marisa or by their words that, nevertheless, unavoidably catch on her ear like a dry branch catching on her dress as she runs past a tree, shunning its protection on a stormy winter night. Gustavo and Marisa's congratulations remain caught on her ears: "Another year and another book. You look radiant!" She can't move forward. Her legs weigh her down, her knees almost buckle as she looks around and around the same faces and the same smiles. But yes, she has shifted. She doesn't know how she got here, leaning on the glass door of the terrace, with a fresh drink in her hand, facing Narcís Soller, who has proposed a sea voyage. Nor does she know with whom she spoke while she was covering the distance or what she said. But unquestionably, she isn't where she was—how much time has gone by?—with Enrique Loreto, whose company she has eluded. No, she wasn't eluding Enrique Loreto, who comes up again. It was the Zumois, especially Alberto, she was avoiding. She has escaped from the publisher's insistent jokes, his supposedly witty remarks. She will try not to exchange another word with Alberto Zumoi for the entire party. What irritated her were his repeated allusions to the reason for this celebration. Yes, she was sailing through the night enclosed in a bell-shaped glass euphoria that was broken by Alberto, that was suddenly smashed to pieces by his booming voice.

It is hot. She should not have accepted Miguel's suggestion—whose gaze she now sees move around the room, meet hers, keep hers fixed while he gives a faint smile, and continue its way until it lights up when it meets Mónica Zumoi's—should not have agreed to organize a party for fifty people, at home, in this heat. Although the Dondis reassure her that "it is a splendid evening; your garden is a delight," she notices their foreheads covered with that other layer of moist, pearly skin that perspiration forms. Young Loreto also insists on denying the oppressive atmosphere of the party. Too many flowers; they wither immediately in the heat, and they stink. They smell like death, she thinks. Or she says it aloud; yes, she does, because she hears herself speaking. She hears her own voice, far away, and Enrique Loreto's: "What an exaggeration! The flowers are holding up wonderfully. And they have such a nice smell! Besides, you have arranged them so skillfully . . . It is that quality of yours, that . . ."

Enrique Loreto's hesitation promises her the imminent verbal expression of a stream of praises. If it were not for the heat, for the oppressive sense of so many people, if it were not for the party and the weariness, perhaps she might help him shorten the preliminaries leading to some idiotic phrase intended to compliment her. But exhaustion prevents her from making the most minimal effort and even stops her from experiencing that feeling of mixed tenderness and sorrow the young man usually inspires in her. Now, as she observes the trembling movement of his masculine hands—thin, with chewed nails—over the waiter's tray from which he lifts two glasses to the level of his own face, she thinks, What tenderness? What pity? She doesn't even feel a liking for the young man who will strive and will manage—with or without her help—to utter all the flattery that he considers opportune and that she considers false and convoluted. Indeed, she hears him continue: "I am referring to the quality you possess that is so, so . . . How can I say it? So genuine in enhancing and indulging the beauty of small things."

She smiles. It is an effort for her to force her lips until she manages the expression most like a smile. She feels how the muscle pulls on her skin. Throughout the party she has repeated the same grimace so much that she doesn't understand what interest—no matter how purely social it may be—the guests can have in causing this grotesque repetition of ceremonial gestures and words. Her mouth will fall off, she fears, from forcing it into feigned expressions of cordiality. Her eyes will fall out from looking at faces like Enrique Loreto's that offer her a monotony incapable of rousing interest. Monotony and repetition. Monotony from repetition. How many young Loretos has she known throughout her fifteen years of marriage? How many fragile Loretos have succeeded one other at her parties? Eight, ten? Some Loreto or other was already present at the fourth or fifth anniversary party, some young poet, a student and fervent admirer of Miguel, who undoubtedly described him to her with the characteristics that he usually attributes to his most sensitive apprentices: "It is necessary to help him, to give him support and attention. He is very intelligent but tremendously unsure and unstable. Be nice to him."

What was the name of the first of those young men who appeared in their lives—in Miguel's and hers—and whose timidity and helplessness went hand in hand with an invincible and stubborn desire to become a regular at their house? During the first visits, it touched her to see how timid and bashful he was. She was moved to pity by the spectacle of his helplessness before a cup of coffee or an interminable drink that remained almost untouched because the young man didn't dare to pick it up and drink: he did not want to extend the trembling evident only in his lips and in the cigarette ash that always fell before it reached the ashtray. During the first interviews, the visitor hardly spoke, and when they were about to draw to a close and no one—neither Miguel nor she—now expected it, the silent, almost monosyllabic young man broke his muteness to fire long speeches about Miguel's poetry that seemed to be recited from an impeccably written draft that took days to memorize. A torture, really; it seemed that beginning to speak amounted to torture for these young men, and then they couldn't stop, and the meticulously developed text lapsed into verbal chaos as it was repeated over and over, with the same words and the same phrases but in a different order as it was recited under the effects of a feverish, pitiful, and alarming excitement revealed like the confusing symptoms of a disease for which the affected person himself states the cure: more time. So the young poet, who was still practically an adolescent, managed not to leave with the feeling that he hadn't said what he had come to say, and in return, he went away having managed to make a new appointment—with a determined and overwhelming insistence that seemed to belie such emotional lack of control—in spite of the embarrassment that overcame him and was evident in everything from the uncontrollable blush and the stammering to his awkward movements as he stumbled toward the door.

"He's oversensitive," Miguel would explain at her initial reaction—a suspicious one, according to him—when she showed a certain displeasure at the puzzling behavior of those young men who combined, in a way both grotesque and moving, an unquestionable prudishness in matters of self-expression and a daring, even rash, stubbornness in imposing their presence. Because it is true that they eventually did impose their presence on the household. Their presence, their admiration, and also—it was necessary to admit it—their affection.

A sincere affection, she now thinks. Yes, the Loretos' affection is sincere; not so deep or lasting as they, the Loretos, believe but, doubtless, genuine for a time. The time it takes to become hatred—if they do not feel that Miguel reciprocates their affection—or contempt—when they discover, or believe they have discovered, that they are capable of writing better than the master or of loving his wife more deeply and with greater sincerity.

Leaning on the glass door to the terrace, she hears herself laugh, not because she agrees with Enrique Loreto's words, as he supposes when he repeats, "It's true, I'm telling you: that quality of yours, so genuine, that is becoming more and more difficult to find in people. . . ," but at her own surprise at thinking about herself as "the master's wife." The master's wife! The poet's muse! as Alberto Zumoi continually exclaims at each toast, pursuing her around the room throughout the entire party, one hand holding a drink and the other brandishing Miguel's new book, dedicated to her as were the previous ten. The muse of the poet and of his followers. How long will it take before Enrique suggests that they go out into the garden so he can hand her a poem addressed to her? she wonders, surprised at the young man's slowness in making a proposal that is daring and decisive for him but predictable and a mere formality for her.

But no, she thinks, it isn't a question of slowness on the young man's part, but of meticulousness. First, he must finish the talk on genuineness dedicated to her; he must finish explaining how important he considers the possession of this innate gift—and he will emphasize the part about innate several times, she predicts, as she observes how the young man's thin hand feels the outside of his dark jacket pocket, assuring himself that he is carrying the poem with him—of this innate gift, he will insist, so difficult to find in people around us even though the tasks they accomplish lead one to suppose just the opposite. He must finish the long, flattering speech before undertaking his feeble, awkward attempt at seduction. Nevertheless, the priority of the flattery is unimportant: it responds neither to an arbitrary sequence of events, only partly carried out, nor—she knows only too well—to a premeditated intention of flattering her at length in order to monopolize her attention and company for a sufficiently protracted space of time to make the eventual visit to the garden a natural extension of the chat they are now having.

No, Enrique's discourse, full of adulation about her genuine qualities, doesn't constitute a selfishly motivated preamble to the exposition of a matter supposedly of paramount importance to him (going out into the garden, delivering a handwritten paper to her with trembling hand as he stammers hasty, barely intelligible phrases, and extracting from her the promise to telephone him after the party, whatever the hour, after having read the poem and the short note that will surely accompany it); his discourse is the essence of the matter: yes, because getting emotional almost to the point of tears as he speaks to her about this genuineness that he has recently invented for her is basically to declare Miguel's falseness.

That declaration, she thinks, is the cause of the emotion that befuddles him and of the voice that breaks as he tries to control it in his desire to shout—not the words supposedly intended to praise her before everyone but the secret intention and obscure origin of those same words: to proclaim Miguel's falseness before everyone there.

This is now and has always been the general direction of the emotional journey of Loreto and his kind, she tells herself: tortuous but basically simple, it leads them to fall in love with her in order to fall out of love with Miguel, or to be more precise, to invent a burning love for her in order to erase the guilt created by the irreversible loathing into which their original adoration for the master has suddenly changed and which claws at their delicate young-poet's conscience; an ardent love that, simply because it is experienced by their sublime artists' spirituality, can demand her reciprocation not for some supposedly innocent purpose, which these Loretos couldn't even conceive apart from Miguel, but rather in their original case against Miguel, a love that can turn into a limpid reflecting mirror of his sentimentality, a spurious sentimentality, as they have recently discovered about their suddenly loathsome teacher. Because the general direction of these Loretos' emotional journeys initially demarcates an ideal space in which to show not that they themselves might possess fascinating abilities in the field of love but that Miguel's are few and false; then it proceeds with the acquisition of the entire construction to which they aspire—a perfect, solid, indestructible edifice that indisputably symbolizes Miguel's falseness, which is not only limited to the ambiguous range of marital feelings but also and above all is present in his literary work. And that devastating critical judgment about the master is all that contains and nourishes the love of these Loretos, she thinks as she hangs on the arm of the flustered young man with the intention of escorting him to some group engaged in general conversation into which she can integrate him and thus get him away, and herself away, from the nearness of the garden and of a scene that at all costs she wants at least to delay, since to avoid it will be practically impossible, given these Loretos' well-known obstinacy.

Because Enrique Loreto, pushing up glasses that regularly slip down his thin nose, eyes fixed on the title page of Miguel's new book as if he were reading for the first time the title of a work he should know by heart, since he has read it from cover to cover during the various stages of its gestation, has now said, "A good title, yes, it is a good title. Miguel's titles are excellent, they are the best thing about his books, don't you think? Well, I'm referring to the latest books; the first ones are something else, more genuine, more . . . I don't mean that the latest ones are bad; of course, you know that I . . . But I don't know, perhaps he has rather imprudently given in to that extraordinary linguistic facility of his, a verbal talent that is undeniable but prone to superficiality. On the other hand, in the early books, perhaps less perfect from a formal point of view—a point which is always highly questionable—there was the throb of a genuine voice, a voice that was more real, more powerful. In short, Miguel may be determined to keep up an excessively fast rhythm of publication. Excessive for a poet, of course. An author of novels, of theater, that's something else. I certainly don't know why he has taken it into his head to write a novel. I think it's a mistake. Of course, if he insists on writing it, he will, and with guaranteed and surely well-deserved success. But why be satisfied with writing a novel that is stylistically good but that, when all is said and done, will be copybook literature that will add nothing new to what has already been written, something he knows perfectly well? Don't you think he wants to take on too much?"

It is imperative to squeeze Enrique Loreto into some conversation group—with a shoehorn, if necessary; it is imperative, she says to herself. Like catching a fly whose buzzing torments us for hours and managing at last to put it inside a carefully corked bottle and then throwing the container far away.

She feels that at this point it would be an impossible undertaking, a boring, exhausting task to relive the intense seesaw of lowly and sublime passions regularly set up between Miguel and his protégé of the moment. It would be like rereading for the eighth, ninth, tenth time a dull, involved novel she knows by heart, a required reading that lasts for several months. To continue listening to Enrique Loreto would now mean starting to read that book, of hypothetical interest only to its characters, Miguel and Loreto, for although the plot might present her as one of the main characters, she knows that she is a mere extra in the story. She has already lived it too many times to believe otherwise. In fact, since the third or fourth year of marriage, when Miguel had already accepted his academic post and had published his second or third book, they have always lived under the shadow of some budding Loreto.

Yes—in fact, almost from the first years, their married life has formed a constant triangle: a triangle in which one of the sides periodically changes its name. No, she thinks, as she hears herself forge a spoken link between Mónica Zumoi and Enrique Loreto ("Mónica, tell Enrique about the scene between Rotellar and Membibres when Gustavo introduced them"); no, it hasn't been a triangle. Her coexistence—what an odd word, she thinks dizzily—with Miguel has formed a square: the professor, the wife, and the duo made up of the favorite disciple in constant disaccord with his plus-or-minus female equivalent. Although to tell the truth, she has stayed on the edge of this domestic geometry. Yes, from the beginning—what beginning, what beginning of what, if she has no memory before this moment, before the dizzying emptiness in which she is falling, sinking, as she sees herself in the mirror and cannot feel within herself the image of that face and that body unrecognizable as her own?—from the beginning of whatever it was, she has not contributed to the formation of any shape, of any combination or structure, be it harmonious or discordant.

She has been a point, an alien element in that game of constructions, like a toy building, which after collapsing time and again recombines the same elements, the same forms and colors, to achieve anew a structural combination identical to the one that has just been taken apart. So one young poet is replaced by another young poet possessing only accidental variants in name and physical characteristics, and one girl—generally beautiful and very well connected socially, determined to find out what lies behind the words and in what way a writer differs from other mortals (as if that difference existed and lay in something secret and intimate that was revealable, because of its subtle nature, only to young people endowed with superior ability)—is replaced by another girl with the identical level of beauty and noble intentions.

Although actually, she thinks, free at last of Enrique Loreto, Miguel is not the one who replaces the two sides of the triangle of which he is the base, but the young apprentice and the beautiful girl who aspires to use up a few golden months of her shining youth in the noble enterprise of attaining sublime knowledge: they are the ones who move away and leave a space, taken up almost immediately by their replacements, as if in compliance with a physical law designed to regulate a closed space, a law that doesn't tolerate a vacuum, that doesn't endure the absence of those elements indispensable for maintaining the integrity of a human combination that works according to the ir-

revocable order of a universe in which the suppression or lack
of one of its astral bodies produces total destruction.

How curious, she says to herself, and how fortunate for
Miguel, that those replacements arrive at the opportune moment, just when one of the positions in the triangle has become
vacant. They seem to come as if summoned by an ad that has
appeared in the newspaper, she thinks, smiling at nothing as she
sits down on one of the sofas, giving in to the tug of Masanés's
hand. He needs an ear—any ear, she reminds herself—for his
deep reflections: "With your sensitivity, with the spirituality that
a poet's wife must have, you will understand me. I was telling
Gustavo that running a bank, a banking group as I do, is work
equivalent to creating a work of art. Think about a concert, for
example. Think about the conductor of an orchestra. On the
one hand, you have the musicians who make up the orchestra,
and the instruments; you have a score—good or bad, you have a
score; you have an audience . . ."

She sinks into the dark red softness of the sofa, as if abandoning
herself to the yielding generosity of an enormous warm body,
next to Masanés the banker, whose profile and half-bald spot
she sees reflected out of the corner of her eye—because she is
pretending to look into his eyes and follow with interest a kind
of shameless monologue that pretends to be a dialogue—in the
mirror situated behind their heads and against the back of the
sofa; in this way, next to Masanés's profile she also sees her own,
her chin slightly tilted so that the rest of her half-face is toward
the back, as if she were trying to protect it from the words and
the breath of her interlocutor, whose short, fat index finger is
now scratching a thin, ginger-colored eyebrow, as if that gesture
could help him find another argument in support of his theory
about the similarity between his banking activities and those
peculiar to art, to any of the arts, or, more exactly—now that he
seems to have exhausted all the examples capable of showing
such a similarity—as if the gesture could help him find a force-
ful argument that might be of use for him to prove, once and

for all, not only an equivalence between his professional dedica-
tion and that of most of the people in the room but also an absolute identity, an identity on which he will expound in terms
that she already knows, because eventually, Masanés unfailingly
rolls out his personal lecture as soon as he has a few more
drinks than usual in the company of those he considers creative
spirits: "It's not about whether finance is like art, but that it is
also an art. An art par excellence, the most difficult and the
most ungrateful. No, no, don't try to console me. I know it, and
what's more, I don't care. But it's ungrateful, very ungrateful,
and lonely, tremendously lonely. Yes, even though no one believes it, mine is one of the most ungrateful, lonely, and un-
selfish professions. Yes, you can understand it and appreciate
the total unselfishness that people like Gustavo are incapable of
seeing in anything that apparently has only practical results. I'll
try to explain that complex issue more clearly . . ."

For that purpose, in order to explain his ideas more clearly
and get to the root of the question, Masanés's index finger
leaves his eyebrow, rises to his almost totally bald head, and remains there for a few seconds during which she still faces the
banker, but instead of looking obliquely at their two profiles in
the mirror behind them to their right, she tilts her face slightly
toward the opposite side, toward the mirror-wall on the left.

At first, she doesn't see herself; she doesn't find herself among
the faces, backs, and reflected flowers. She doesn't find her face
in the surface that is getting more and more misty with smoke
and diffuse colors and that reproduces the entire company in the
room plus the images of the same group reflected in the opposite mirror. The entire group, except for her, as if she were not
there. It calms her not to see herself, to have this visual proof of
not being where she is, and just as she considers herself absent,
she suddenly sees, in the far mirror, her hand and her arm in
the air, Masanés's round, flushed face, his hand placing a drink
in hers, which withdraws, recoils. And when the movement of
someone in the room alters the images in the mirror, she
watches the backward movement of her bent elbow, of her arm,

of her hand, and of the drink until she sees a face she knows and to which she mechanically directs a smile that freezes, unfinished and absurd, as she recognizes the face she is greeting as her own. A frightened bird's small, sharp face, about to become detached from a stiff body, a bird perched rather than seated comfortably, ready to take off in confused flight, with no direction or fixed objective.

What a strange contradiction there is, she tells herself, between the feeling that she has of herself, when she doesn't see herself, and the view of the external person that the mirror provides. What a difference between feeling herself and seeing herself. It is like imagining and, at the same time, seeing the two farthest points on a road that leads not to the joining of those points but to their divergence, to their absolute, irremediable, and somewhat painful disconnection, since the road turns into an absurd, senseless gash in heaven-knows-what kind of rugged landscape once it loses its function of establishing a logical relationship between the opposite points that make it up: the inner perception of herself and the outer one, how she feels herself and how she sees herself; a feeling and an image that do not agree and that—since she experiences one and sees the other, but separately—produce in her the dizzy sensation of being two but also of not being any.

If she stops looking at herself in the mirror, she feels as if she is spread out on the sofa; her mouth feels hard, made of stone, unfit to utter any precise phrase; her eyes feel dull, her lids swollen. On the other hand, the mirror shows her sitting lightly and rather straight on the edge of the sofa, poised for sudden, agile motion; it shows her lips moving continually between a smile and a word; it shows her dark, lively eyes wide open, with no trace of swelling although they are fixed, too fixed, as if riveted on what they see. That, she says to herself, is what makes her look like a frightened bird about to take flight—from the cold or from some unexpected danger.

But it isn't cold. And all through the party, the only surprise is suddenly seeing herself with a surprised expression because she finds herself there, looking at herself, at a party. The party for the fifteenth anniversary of their marriage. Fifteen years is part of a lifetime. A lifetime. But after all, what is a lifetime? she thinks. And right away, she tells herself that it is better not to think about it, not to think. Take another drink and breathe deeply. Although actually, she doesn't think, she never thinks, she tells herself. And the urgent, self-imposed order (don't think, no, not tonight) is designed to deflect not concrete thoughts but phrases, only phrases that suddenly fall on her consciousness with the overwhelming, disconcerting weight of fruit that has fallen from a tree in a sterile orchard. They are only short phrases that suddenly burst loudly inside her head and announce a subject for possible reflection that nevertheless does not take place. Because the clarity of the phrase, or perhaps only the fact of its spoken presence in her consciousness, crushingly underscores the absolute emptiness of the mind that receives it. She doesn't mean to reject the act of thinking itself but the recognition of that mental emptiness against which any word, any phrase enclosed in her thought collides and rebounds as if, struggling to continue or even to find a possible meaningful connection, it had discovered nothing but this emptiness as an echo. An emptiness that physically ingests her: it swallows her and everything near her and then deposits the crushed remains in the pit of her stomach, where it eructs in sharp spasms and stifles her breathing.

The phrases must be stopped, she tells herself, not the nonexistent thought. The unsummoned phrases that arrive suddenly and settle in her head, where they repeat themselves with an insistence that does not lead to their uncontrolled multiplication or to coherent reflection but to mere repetition. One or two phrases usually alternate evenly, or more frequently, one repeats itself countless times, and when it seems about to die out, it alternates with two or three repetitions of the other one. So, she thinks—no, she doesn't think, she hears—What is a lifetime? What is, after all, a lifetime? And she hears it one, ten, twenty times, until the repetition is interrupted by another phrase, *Elle*

est retrouvée. Quoi? L'Eternité. And her thought, her only voluntary thought (stop, stop the phrases, don't think; she has no
wish to know just what a lifetime is or to find out where these
verses are coming from: she doesn't know the writer or at what
period in her life she read them) doesn't manage to halt the repetition of the question followed by the illogical answer in an al-
ternation certainly favorable to the question over the answer, at
least for the moment, and at an irregular speed that fluctuates
between throbbing rhythm and a soporific sluggishness, the
one predisposing her to anxiety, and the other, to immobility
and to the unawareness of external stimuli that is typical of
sleep.

But she must make an effort, she tells herself, she must give
up sleep and make an effort to endure the rest of the party. The
rest of the party and its conclusion. Because what she dreads especially about the large dinner parties she gives at home is the
end. Even though when she wakes up in the mornings, assailed
by the crushing certainty that she won't be able to endure the
beginning of the gathering planned for that evening and cannot
remember that her morning inertia invariably disappears in the
end with the first drinks and the first guests to arrive and then
slips away quickly, delightfully, over the soft wave formed by the
rippling start of the party, actually, what she can't bear is the end
of these parties. She doesn't recall any pleasant end of a party.
They go on and on. Yes, now that she thinks about the end of
large gatherings, she retains the painful feeling of drifting from
guest to guest, each the same, standing and creating a maze of
paths in a living room that by the end of the evening she defi-
nitely does not recognize as her own.

After the radiant beginning of the party, why does the euphoria of the first drinks disappear, why does she allow herself to be
overcome by anxiousness to get to the end as soon as possible,
to drink up the three, four hours of the party in the briefness of
one long swallow, of one meaningless remark? Why this anxiety
to get to the end of the party if—she knows—she hates the ends
of parties, always longer than the parties themselves? Why does

she prolong them, why does she always insist on detaining the first guest to leave and do it not motivated by simple courtesy but by a genuine wish not to dampen this celebration which is turning out to be so . . . so. . . ?

And from far away, her own cheerful voice seems strange, unfamiliar, like the friend who allows himself to be detained, like the group of guests who are laughing at the witticism of— Miguel? who puts his arm around her shoulders; he seems as animated and fresh as if he had just arrived at the party, compared to her . . . Where does he get the strength to improvise witty remarks about matters that don't interest him in the least, while she feels about to cry and shriek because the night, increasingly dark, is about to explode behind the windows that look out onto the terrace and the trays with the remains of fruit and sweets, the empty bottles barely concealed behind the hydrangeas. Oh, she detests having to tell them again and again to remove the bottles as they are emptied. She can't bear to see them empty. They perforate her stomach; their broken fragments pierce her breast. And the flowers, too, those flowers don't let her breathe deeply. They are losing color. No, they aren't fading; on the contrary, the blue of the hydrangeas is deepening and the yellow of the narcissus too, but they don't get brighter; the intensity of the color deepens, and they darken. The faces also darken. Cigarette smoke dulls the dry colors of flowers and faces that seem to be reproduced by a bad painter rather than by the steamy surfaces of the mirrors. A bad painter like Mario Peral, for example, with whom she is sharing a newly uncorked bottle and to whose theories on the death of nonfigurative art Miguel pretends to listen attentively and to corroborate verbally ("Yes, yes, you are right, it was a bad dream, a nightmare that was absolutely good for nothing"), while his narrowed and now somewhat reddened eyes move restlessly behind his glasses, sweeping the room in a search that seems to end when his gaze stops at Mónica Zumoi's face, as if she were the object of his frugal optic quest, but after the first stage of the search, it continues until it comes across Enrique Loreto, and when it discovers him, the search does indeed end, but only to begin again, because after his glance meets Enrique's, it returns to a possible meeting with Mónica's; in fact, she waits only a few seconds before turning her face toward him, smiling at him from a distance, and as if following the force of the triangular imperative, her head begins a rotation that doesn't even get half-way through the three hundred sixty degrees suggested by the rapidity with which she started the movement, because she has hardly begun when her smile freezes, then widens—exagger-atedly, she thinks, compared with the way Mónica smiled at Miguel—when it meets Enrique Loreto's, who, still looking back and forth between Mónica and Miguel, tries to leave Mem-bribes's company and moves forward a few steps in the direc-tion of the place in the room where Mónica is; and, as Mem-bribes's feet follow the movement of his interlocutor's, both of them—one deliberately and the other rather mechanically—move with slow but uninterrupted steps toward Mónica. Mem-bribes is not aware—but Enrique Loreto is indeed—that Mi-guel, after freeing himself from Mario Peral and his opinions about the latest providential crisis in avant-garde art, makes his way toward them but will not manage to join them because on his way toward Mónica Matilda waylays him.

Anyone there who might have intercepted his journey to-ward the sofa where Mónica and Loreto are about to sit down would have annoyed Miguel, she thinks, automatically smiling in sympathy. But that it was none other than Matilda plunges him into a confusion bordering on anguish for which he has no ready defense and which he indicates solely by—she knows the gesture only too well—clamping his teeth on the mouthpiece of his pipe, with one hand on the bowl and the other deep in his pants pocket as he leans his long torso forward as if he were going to break in two. Any other person who might have cut off his progress toward those two young apples of his eye—an increasingly impelling progress that is complicated when the other two, or one of them, leaves the place where they are as soon as he is about to reach it—would not have received the same consideration as Matilda, to whom Miguel must continue paying attention even though in fact he has been avoiding her for some time.

If it were not for Matilda's well-known prudence, for her reliability in dealing with those who know her well, for the wisdom and delicacy she brings to her relationship with people of whom she is fond, Miguel's state of mind, she thinks, would be closer to suffering right now than to discomfort. Although, in fact, he is suffering, she tells herself when she notices his pale, slightly greenish face in the mirror facing the sofa on which she is sitting, apparently relaxed at last, and which is located behind Miguel and facing Matilda, who offers him an open, unconstrained smile.

One could have foreseen, she thinks, that Matilda would decide to approach Miguel, to be the one to take his arm and talk to him as if nothing had happened between them, thus putting an end to the other's ridiculous avoidance. Yes, she tells herself, she will do it frankly, without insinuations, without veiled explanations, and without calling for them either. And, after more than twenty years of deep friendship with Matilda, Miguel knows that there won't be any, that it is better not to have any. At least for the moment. Because Matilda's best explanation, the most sincere and friendly one up to the moment when one asks her for an explanation, is silence. Silence at the opening of Miguel's latest play, silence at the housewarming for Miguel's enormous new house, silence at Miguel's simultaneous, brilliant career as an academician, silence at the examples of the poetry by Miguel's young, talented discoveries, silence at Miguel's multiple extraliterary activities to finance artistic projects with the economic support of people before whom Matilda allows Miguel to show her off but to whom she offers only silence.

Matilda's silence during the last—how many?—years, she thinks, is the only mirror into which Miguel can look without seeing himself distorted by the play of lights, whether they be flattering or distorting, that a life of quick, unexpected successes projects onto any surface or reflecting environment. This is the reason for the dread that Matilda's silence causes him, a silence he avoids like the worst censure because it gives him back his current image completely bare, stripped of the person he used to be twenty years ago.

Yet what does she know, in fact, about Matilda's silence, about the reasons behind her attitude? What can she know, she tells herself, sitting at an anniversary party, watching Miguel and his interlocutor from an unreal distance measurable only according to the changing rules of senses influenced more by mental vagaries than by tangible surroundings? What does she know of Matilda's thoughts? Why should she attribute opinions and thoughts to Matilda that. . . ? No, they aren't Matilda's, and they are not her own, either. Because she doesn't think, she never has thought. Never. She has always been nothing but air penetrated by a series of disjointed images in which she doesn't appear. Nothing but air, penetrated by others' phrases heard inside her empty head, sometimes accompanied by the fleeting glimpse of the book to which they belong or of the person who utters them. But Matilda has never expressed any opinion about Miguel aloud. And as for herself, what does she know about Miguel? What does she know of the Miguel who celebrates wedding anniversaries and book publications and of the Miguel from twenty years ago? No, she doesn't want to think about the Miguel from twenty years ago or about herself. Even if she wanted to, she couldn't. She can't remember herself before now. Just a brief view of a tree-lined avenue that disappears into a green distance and the vague sensation of her skin walking along it: the feel of the houses and the road brushing against her body, a luminous, shining sky, an azure brilliance that explodes through the branches of the trees and takes her breath away. Nothing more. There is no more. Then, perhaps, sometimes, the sea—white, wintry pale, filling the faded screen of her memory, but now without her. She no longer sees herself. And voices— yes, voices, repeating themselves. *Elle est retrouvée. Quoi? L'Eternité.* But not knowing their source or to whom they belong. Like now, a moment ago, when she thought she perceived Matilda's opinions about Miguel's career path without Matilda's ever having expressed any views on that subject. She put herself in Matilda's mind, just like that. It frequently happens that she suddenly finds herself in someone's mind. They are sympathetic transfers, Andrés used to say. Oh, but not now, she is determined not to think about Andrés now. Why remember him now, after so many years, just on the verge of a party's end— dangerous, loathed, like all ends of all parties? Andrés. She didn't see Andrés's young, lean form crushed in the middle of the road also fifteen years ago today. She didn't see it. Nevertheless, occasionally—never intentionally—since that time, the imagined picture has appeared before her eyes like a false memory. A fleeting sight she has immediately rejected and, more urgently than voluntarily, replaced with the real memory of the last time she saw Andrés sitting on the terrace of a bar: resplendent in his light-colored suit, legs imperiously crossed, the suggestion of an affectionate smile on his beautiful face with perfect features ("Everything about him is perfect," Miguel said in annoyance, "like the career he will follow, the children he will have, the houses and cars that. . ."), his half-closed eyes avoiding the glaring light of a summer sun, and one hand elegantly raised in a gesture of farewell as she left—oh yes, full of doubts, always full of doubts—to go and meet Miguel. If she hadn't answered Miguel's urgent summons, if she had stayed there, on that terrace with Andrés . . . But why think about Andrés now? Yes, it was the verses, she tells herself, *Elle est retrouvée. Quoi? L'Eternité.* Andrés was the one who read them, the one who gave her the little volume of poems bound in green leather ("You must admit that he is a phony," Miguel said in exasperation. "How can poetry interest a budding economist?"). Yes, it was Andrés. And she, who never remembers anything, who is incapable of retaining a phrase or the sense of a conversation held only a week ago, why does she remember it precisely today? It was the verses, she tells herself, and her sympathetic transfers, what Andrés would call her sympathetic transfers. Her ability to be with someone and attribute thoughts to him that, in general, she

shares. Or no, she doesn't share them. She accepts them without subjecting them to any consideration at all. Transformed
inevitably, inescapably into the receptacle of a natural phenomenon, she receives them like rain that falls during a dream and
gives the dreamer only the image of rain on his face but not the
feeling of its impact on his skin, or like real rain on the insensi-
ble face of a person who is awake and passing through no one's
dream. Yes, it is an old phenomenon for her: opening her mind
to thoughts sketched out in someone else's and allowing them
to enter and remain in her own consciousness without its un-
dergoing the least alteration, as if, in some vague corner of her
no less vague private self, she allowed the installation of scenery
for a drama in whose plot development she took part neither as
an author nor as a simple extra. Or, she tells herself, perhaps the
opposite may happen; perhaps her thought is the occasional
guest in someone else's mind, as it was a few moments ago in
Matilda's, and then proceeds to meditations that in hers . . . But
that's not right, because she doesn't think. And now she doesn't
even remember what kind of thoughts she has just attributed to
Matilda or why Miguel has interrupted his pursuit of Mónica
Zumoi and Enrique Loreto toward whom he has been making
his way since heaven knows how long.

But, she thinks, the dance will go on. The movements of the
three dancers through the room, looking for each other and
avoiding each other among the guests, will continue creating invisible scalene spaces, isosceles forms contingent on Miguel's
determination to approach Mónica or Enrique Loreto and con-
ditional upon the determination of one of them to move away
from the master and if possible drag the other one off as a way
of rejecting him. And here she is, she tells herself, alien as always
to the triangular ensemble but looking at it from the outside,
alert to the development of a game not shared but whose end
she foresees, to judge from Loreto's cutting remarks throughout
the party and from Mónica's obvious and repeated refusal to assume the hosting duties of the party with Miguel, which she has
usually shared, more or less surreptitiously, during the last year

and a half. An imminent finale, as the lit-up window in the library indicates, she tells herself, suddenly startled as her hand brushes Mónica's and she finds herself sitting next to Mónica in the garden, for how long she does not know, and feels herself caught between the gaze of those light-colored eyes and Enrique Loreto's nervous smalltalk about the drawbacks of success when it comes to maintaining the necessary rigor in carrying out any artistic task.

How has she reached this point, this bench in the garden and this company—Mónica Zumoi's and Enrique Loreto's—increasingly unwanted as the party has progressed? How much time has she spent in the middle of the bench flanked by the two young people whose presence, like ghostly apparitions that startle you in the dead of night, she has just discovered? How many guests have left already? she calculates, turning her gaze toward the living room, an idle, futile gaze that remains caught on the panes of the terrace door, through which it can't pass in its mission to report on the interior of the room where she can get only an out-of-focus glimpse of half a dozen stragglers, acquaintances whom she doesn't recognize. Did she say goodbye to the others? Did Miguel do it before going up to the library? Because she places him with absolute certainty in the library, on account of its lit-up window.

The light from the floor above was the first stimulus her senses perceived when she woke up, when she emerged from a total unconsciousness that had lasted she had no idea how long; the light in the library window, the coolness of the night, the scent of jasmine, the faint voices an agreeable distance away in the living room. Or was it the voices of her unwanted companions that dragged her from a dream she does not want to relinquish? The voices of Mónica and Enrique Loreto plus—oh no! Alberto Zumoi is with her again, uncorking a bottle. She accepts a drink but not the invitation to join in a conversation that unfolds in her presence, a conversation she hears and intends to continue hearing from the other side of the swell of drowsiness that rocks her and carries her along as if her whole being were an enormous, clumsy cork. She is all cork. Especially her head. Also her arms and legs, which she scarcely feels and can't move to carry out a violent, powerful desire that has been hidden deep in her consciousness for hours and from which it is about to burst with the same force as the stopper of the bottle uncorked by Alberto: to interrupt abruptly this little gathering of stragglers out there in the open, to leave the damned party and disappear into the bedroom without saying goodbye to the few guests still remaining in the living room; to climb to the upper floor in the dark and go to bed at last, without seeing anyone, without speaking to anyone, to lie down on the bed without wasting time getting undressed and to hurl herself into the white, total emptiness of a deep, leaden sleep. But now she is all cork. A great soundless cork, that's what her head feels like. She can't rise and get to the living room — covering — how many yards of distance? she wonders — although she knows it is only a few steps negotiable with an abrupt act of will easy to put into practice as soon as she decides to do so. As soon as she decides to do so, she repeats to herself, recapturing the memory of the ends of other parties. Yes, as soon as she decides to do so, she will stand up, and hardly aware of the effort made, she will find herself in the room that, from the garden, looks like an illuminated rectangular box. It disgusts her to enter there for fear of being shut up inside it again and not being able to continue her way toward the upper floor. Although, she tells herself, if she managed not to be held up in the living room by any of the guests, whose outlines she can make out indistinctly, and could get to the upper floor at last, before reaching the door to her room, she would have to pass by the library where Miguel is looking for the book. No, she tells herself, he won't find it. The light on in the library for so long leads her to assume that as usual Miguel cannot find the book he is looking for. How many times has he bought *Dubliners*? How many times has this book, so important in Miguel's emotional life, gotten lost? Perhaps it would be useful, in order to conclude as soon as possible, to go up herself to look for the book, because Mónica is waiting — as she is explaining to Alberto in answer to the insistent "I'll wait for you inside so we can leave"—for Miguel to return with a book he promised to lend her. Nevertheless, how does she know what would be more helpful? She has had too much to drink, she reproaches herself, and from the disconnected phrases exchanged between Mónica and Alberto Zumoi she can't guess if the young woman's vacillations hide her intention to stay behind, without Alberto, and wait for Miguel; to leave with Enrique; to continue waiting for Miguel with Enrique, letting Alberto leave alone or . . . But Enrique Loreto, with the brusqueness that characterizes him once he overcomes his young-artist clumsiness and hesitancies, is the one who nullifies the entire range of doubts by imposing his decision to be the one to go off with Alberto. And, on the other side of the blurry lens formed by her half-closed eyes, she sees Enrique Loreto finally leaving a party, arm in arm with a publisher.

She manages to choke back a hysterical laugh. Seen from behind, somewhat timid next to the confident Zumoi, and spluttering faltering praises on his companion's work as a publisher, Loreto inspires pity in her; he gives her the disagreeable feeling of a compassion she has already felt. And she hates to feel pity. She has had too much to drink, she tells herself, draining another glass. Her head is spinning, and she feels a lump in her throat. She closes her eyes, hoping that, when she opens them again, she will see that the light in the library window has finally been turned off and that the place next to her that Mónica now occupies will be empty. This will obviously prove that Miguel has found the book. Will he give it to Mónica, as he gave it to her, almost twenty years ago, and ask her to read Joyce's "The Dead" that very night? "I won't bother you any more. It is the last thing I'll ask of you." But the Miguel from those days— the humble, tall, gawky student dressed in a raveling sweater, with yellowish nails and dark, badly shaved skin—that young suicidal poet inspired pity in her. And Andrés? She has had too much to drink, she repeats to herself. Why remember Andrés now, if she almost never thinks of him or of his death, which also took place fifteen years ago today, or of Miguel asking her to read "The Dead"? No, she tries not to think, tries to remember nothing, absolutely nothing. Otherwise, a lump constricts her throat and an old sorrow fills her eyes with tears. Not for her, not for Miguel, not for Andrés. It is an old anxiety, like the one she feels when she puts a hand in her pocket and discovers an object that doesn't belong to her. That's enough, she says to herself. She has had too much to drink. She hates anniversaries. Fifteen years. Almost a lifetime. But, after all, what is a lifetime? she wonders; what is it but a whirlpool stirred up around her by strange, completely alien currents that ceaselessly make her dizzy but never sweep her away. What does she know of this whirlpool and of those caught in it, except for the old feeling of pity that renders her incapable of understanding them? That's enough, she repeats to herself, that's enough. Tomorrow she will wake up sick. She has had too much to drink. How incredible that she can still stand up, she thinks, as she sees herself in the mirrors of the room, as she crosses it, goes toward the door to say goodby to some friends of friends whose names she pretends to remember by not saying them, and continues on to the upper floor. She almost gropes her way across the hall. The bedroom walls whirl dizzily before she falls into bed, and she has to force her eyes to look at the doorframe where Miguel appears; without giving him time to answer, she forces her furry mouth and tongue to say to him, "On the third shelf to the right, but in your study, not in the library." She thinks that Mónica probably has read "The Dead" — she vaguely remembers having heard her say so once — but she doesn't tell Miguel, who mumbles a soft "Thanks," leaves the bedroom, returns again, stands for a few seconds in silence, hesitantly, then whispers words that receive an answer from her that neither of them can remember.

AFTERWORD

by Margaret E. W. Jones

When the noted critic José María Castellet published *Nueve novísimos poetas españoles* (Nine of the newest Spanish poets) in 1970, Ana María Moix was the only woman represented in the groundbreaking anthology. Castellet's introduction of Moix to the Hispanic literary community deals with her poetry and not the prose for which she is best known today; he includes her because she is part of a group of writers whose generational affinities transcend genre. Most of the *novísimos* were born roughly a decade after the Spanish civil war of 1936–39 (Moix was born in 1947). Their early years were spent under the dictator Francisco Franco's regime, in which the partnership of state and church set an archconservative policy of political and social conformity and in which censorship assured compliance of the media. Increasingly liberal policies of the 1960s and early 1970s heralded the dizzying changes that would occur after Franco's death in 1975. Political unrest, a socialist government, renewed civil rights, women's issues, and the celebration of regional differences were some of the milestones in an age of shifting national priorities. Uncensored expression encouraged a frenzy of creative activity and publishing. In addition to these changes, Spanish and international popular culture—comics, movies, popular music (including rock)—which had flourished in spite of government control, permeated the literature of the *novísimos* and became a statement of their generational and artistic concerns. They are confrontational, sarcastic, demythifying, ambiguous in tone; stylistic and thematic innovations distance the reader from the text. Castellet explains that these writings represent "la ruptura"—a deliberate break—from previous literary and cultural traditions that in general were grounded in contemporary reality and often contained a social message.

Moix shares the stylistic and thematic interests of her fellow *novísimos.* Nevertheless, her unique creative talent is evident in brilliant reworkings of themes that have intrigued her for over twenty-five years of creative activity.[1] Her writing captures an atmosphere of disillusionment and anxiety, a fundamental lack of integration with the world and with one's own self-image. An early statement by Moix, deceptively entitled "Poética" (About my poetry), anticipates this bleak view. Less a literary manifesto than an autobiographical statement, it acknowledges the inter-dependence of literature and life: "We [my brothers Terenci and Miguel and I] didn't know anything about life; we had learned everything from books, comics, movies, and songs. Miguel died without having had time to find out if there was any difference, so I dedicate these poems to him; they prove that there isn't any difference."[2] These words anticipate the constant interplay among language, text, and life in Moix's works and her growing preoccupation with the primacy of language. They also fore-shadow the vision of an increasingly impenetrable world that adds a note of postmodern instability to her work.

Two books of poetry inaugurated her literary career: *Baladas del dulce Jim* (Ballads of sweet Jim) and *Call Me Stone* (1969); *No Time for Flowers y otras historias* followed two years later, for which she received a prize (the Premio Vizcaya del Ateneo de Bilbao). Her obsession with the past and memory, loneliness and escape, the tongue-in-cheek admixture of dissonant elements (Che Guevara playing cards with the nineteenth-century Romantic poet Bécquer), images from popular culture, the overlap of the real and the imaginary—these themes place an unmistakable stamp on her poems. Experimentation with form and language initiates an ongoing attempt to flout literary conventions.

In 1969, Moix turned to prose, publishing two substantial novels and a book of short stories within the space of three years. In *Julia* (1970), a young woman reviews her life during one long night after an unsuccessful suicide attempt. As her remembrances peel away the layers of her past, she reveals chilling details of a life filled with alienation and unhappiness. Her family is dysfunctional; her attempts to bond with her mother and other women are thwarted; her reaction to the conformity of the Catalan middle class is defiant. Then she discloses a key event from her childhood: when she was six, she was raped by a family friend. This traumatic, repressed experience is partly responsible for her obsession with the past.

Next, a book of short stories appeared, and then *Walter, ¿por qué te fuiste?* (Walter, why did you leave?, 1973). Several elements link this novel to *Julia:* they share some of the same characters (now widened to a family of cousins), the class system with its hypocritical, normative values, the resultant alienation and maladjustment, a sense of disillusionment and loss, and the emphasis on the past and on memory. The frame tale describes Ismael's return to the deserted family vacation home of his childhood in search of his cousin Lea, to whom he is to deliver a packet of letters from Julia, who has died in a sanatorium. Several narrative voices recall adventures and relationships from bygone days, particularly the young cousins' fascination with the rebellious Lea, a nonconformist who fires their imaginations with descriptions of her mysterious friend Walter. Ismael discovers that this mythic figure is not a dashing hero but an uninteresting seminarian whom Lea is diabolically trying to seduce.

Eroticism becomes a dominant note. Sex is part of the maturation process, a symbol of defiance and freedom, and a means of psychological manipulation. Cinema and popular music obsess the children, who see them as forms of rebellion and escape. Increasingly complex stylistic devices enrich the novel: multiple narrative strands, intertextuality, metafiction, and some unusual surrealistic touches (a character who is half woman and half horse).

The ten stories in *Ese chico pelirrojo a quien veo cada día* (That red-headed boy I see every day, 1971) illustrate Moix's continuing experimentation and a playful virtuosity. A conformist, hypocritical society provides an unpleasant backdrop for characters who range from bewildered children to maladjusted, unhappy adults. Perplexity, alienation, and even madness result from limitations that stifle the ideals and aspirations of the characters. An indictment of the patriarchal treatment of women and the insistent theme of sexuality link these stories to the novels. Irony, bitter humor, and techniques of disruption carefully orchestrate the narrative flow and control the reader's reaction to the psychological or personal dilemmas of the characters.

Over a decade elapsed before Moix's next book of fiction appeared. While struggling with alcoholism and depression, she had turned her attention to other kinds of discourse: children's literature, translations, a book of interviews, and other nonfictional works.[3] During this period, she was also associated with *Vindicación feminista,* an important feminist journal with a mission to report on national and international issues from a feminist point of view. Among other things, it offered articles on social, legal, and political concerns; features on matters of particular interest to women (divorce, abuse, economic exploitation, etc.); and information on feminist organizations and on noteworthy women of achievement. During the short life of this journal (1976–79), Ana María Moix served as cultural coordinator; reviewed books, movies, and other events; and contributed a regular column entitled "Nena no t'enfilis: Diario de una hija de familia" (Behave yourself, young lady: Diary of a dutiful daughter), a witty "chronicle" in which a young woman describes life in her middle-class household. Caricature and stereotype ridicule the traditional bourgeois family structure and its values, but the amusing sketches contain serious indictments of the standards that circumscribe a woman's life during that period. The deliberately light tone distinguishes this column from the militant stance of most of the material in *Vindicación feminista,* but it accurately reflects Moix's own views: although in agreement with the principles of feminism, she does not consider herself to be a militant feminist; she prefers a less confrontational approach to women's issues, which explains in part the way she develops this theme in her literature. Rather than impose a preconceived conceptual framework on a literary piece, Moix permits the ideology to arise as a natural part of the creative process.[4]

Moix's most recent work presents her ongoing exploration of the possibilities of literary form. *Vals negro* (Black waltz, 1994) was originally intended as a historical biography of Elizabeth, empress of the Austro-Hungarian Empire, but as the work evolved, Moix realized that fiction was a better medium to express the tragedy of this nineteenth-century figure. Several narrative voices and a touch of the fantastic add a poignant dimension to this account of the unhappy woman's life and death.

Dangerous Virtues first appeared in 1985 as *Las virtudes peligrosas* and won the Ciudad de Barcelona prize. Although the stories in this collection seem unrelated at first glance, several elements bind them into a close ideological relationship. Moix's choice of material and the unusual focalization (the perspective from which the events are presented) of the pieces refine ideas that were latent in her earlier works, not the least of which is an underlying nihilism that seems to drive the stories.[5] Plot emphasis moves from process (the development and maturation of the adolescent, a hitherto key theme) to a terrible kind of stagnation, in which the "action" unfolds on an interior plane. Most of the characters are completely static; their lack of development or change merely emphasizes their hopelessness. An aura of failure or despair complements their inability to resolve the tension stemming from a conflict between desire and reality.

The internal focalization in several stories allows unmediated access to the characters' feelings of unhappiness and alienation, and it creates a sense of terrible isolation. The use of free indirect discourse, which slides between first and third person, underlines the ambiguity of the text and emphasizes the tension between interior and exterior (a device particularly evident in "The Dead"). This narrative perspective creates a break between the characters and their environment, between reality and appearances, or between the conscious and the subconscious world.

A deliberately hermetic text destroys the comfortable parallels with the reader's world, reinforcing the impression of solitude and helplessness. Reality seems to lose its permanent characteristics; empirical evidence is unreliable. Conflicting sources show the perplexing relativity of all things and the impossibility of solutions or answers. By replacing facts and explanations, ambiguity and allusion subvert the mimetic reflection of everyday life. The plot development downplays linearity of action and time, undermining cause and effect; neither concrete references to time and setting nor physical descriptions of characters receive much attention. As these conventional parallels with reality are dropped, the text becomes increasingly abstract.

The style in all the stories is deliberately self-conscious. Long, complex sentences, striking images, recondite vocabulary, occasional tongue-in-cheek touches or comic (even tragicomic) notes retard identification with the circumstances and create an aesthetic barrier that brings to the foreground language and text as process. Verbal ambiguities underscore the slippery nature of reality: both subjects and thoughts blend seamlessly into one another, often without transition. In the title story, Moix even delays identifying the narrator, using a disembodied voice to produce a narrative tension that subtly echoes the problematic existence of the characters.

A fascination with the gaze and attendant visual themes also unites *Dangerous Virtues:* the metaphor of sight appears in all the stories in different guises. Variations of spying, watching, and gazing fill these pages: the most obvious are the glances exchanged by the women, the voyeurism of the general and his son, and Alice's prying in "Dangerous Virtues" and *Only One Left to Tell It*'s responsibilities of surveillance in "Once upon a Time." Images of reflection, which suggest the self-gaze and for which the mirror is the single most prevalent symbol, are scattered throughout the text. The women gazing into each other's eyes in "Dangerous Virtues" symbolize human reflection; their ecstatic visual union degenerates into the inanimate facing portraits and finally into mirrors covered with black veils as if in mourning. Even Alice's non-Spanish name suggests the curious girl in Lewis Carroll's *Through the Looking Glass.* In "The Problem," an existential dilemma impels the Problem to enter the

mirror, but his comically failed suicide suggests that enlighten-
ment (especially self-knowledge) is beyond our grasp. Even the
smug protagonist of "The Naive Man" must acknowledge his
degradation when he sees himself in the barroom mirror. "The
Dead" contains the most unsettling use of the mirror image: the
two huge mirror-walls transform an anniversary party into a
surreal nightmare of protean, nonhuman figures; since the mirrors face each other, they multiply the scenes and displace reality into the visually repetitive images that intensify the dizziness
that the protagonist experiences.

The influence of the cinema (another variation on the visual
theme) is detectable in the stories. Although there are few direct
references (e.g., the Disney movies such as *Snow White and the
Seven Dwarfs*), there are parodic resonances of specific films
(see n. 11) or stock scenes from popular culture (the drunk unburdening himself in the bar). Moix borrows filmic techniques
to unfold the characters' obsessive reappraisal of the past. The
written word metamorphoses into film clips, snapshots, freeze-
frames, or other pictorial devices; the characters watch their
own past as a spectacle that memory puts into motion and that
they can view and review. The opening paragraph of the book
adopts the filmic mode as Alice is told to "show the film that
our senses make" and "have your mental projector rewind that
film"; the young man's review of his behavior in "The Naive
Man" and the woman's recollections of time spent with her
children in "The Dead" turn the past into an album filled with
visual memories.

Intertextuality forges thought-provoking links with other
works: the title *Dangerous Virtues* recalls Laclos's *Les liaisons
dangereuses;* the conventions of children's tales form the basis
for "Once upon a Time." "The Dead" refers the reader to a story
of the same name in James Joyce's *Dubliners:* a noisy party
opens a tale that also treats the lack of communication between
a married couple, unexpressed feelings, a mirror encounter, and
ghosts of the past ruled by memories of a dead lover. Moix fills
these stories with direct or oblique references (in "The Dead,"

for example, the unidentified French verses that repeat themselves in the protagonist's mind are from *Une saison en enfer* by Arthur Rimbaud; references to the "drunken boat" are inspired by another Rimbaud work, *Le bateau ivre*). And in a brilliant parody of the very device that she uses so seriously, Moix also mocks and subverts the conventions of intertextuality by inventing the romantic novel from which Alice quotes and by making frequent references to motifs in "Once upon a Time" as if they were well known (the bungling fairy godmother, the hanged man's tree, Count Laurel's motto, etc.).[6]

Moix also uses literary devices to illustrate existential problems. Techniques of metafiction explore the role one is expected to play in life—or that one would wish to play.[7] The characters in "Once upon a Time" are unchangeable literary models, and on a more subtle level, the Problem's problem is his dissatisfaction with his lot in life. "The Naive Man" and "The Dead" contain references to life as a boring book into which the characters have been written without their consent; "The Dead" constantly alludes to stage sets and role playing to underline the unhappy situation. Metafiction both complements and explains the characters' lack of development or inability to effect change: there is no way to rewrite or erase the words that determine their role in life.

Intertextuality (through reference to literature or to popular culture) complements this metafiction; in turn, metafictional motifs (roles, scripts, books) allow Moix to work out the metaphor to its unhappy conclusion: the reduction of life to a role, to phrases, to isolated words, and finally to nothing. Allusions to writing, diaries, and actual texts draw the reader into the metafictional whirl; the device of the mirror simply corroborates the reflection as meaningless repetition. The self-conscious text suggests that this fictional world is a reflector of yet another artifice.

"Dangerous Virtues," the title story, is a brilliant example of how Moix inserts ideas of subversion and disruption into the plot, then subtly emphasizes them through narrative strategy.

Mysterious events, allusive comments, and an open ending leave the reader unsettled, bewildered. The highly charged episodes of the drama unfold at an unspecified time and place, and the main participants are never named. The mutual attraction of the two beautiful women is extraordinary in every sense of the word: their unusual relationship seems limited to chance meetings at which they wordlessly stare at each other. The husband of one of them—the strategist general—has a patriarchal intolerance for any deviation from established norms of behavior. His love of logic and order and his faith in the rational world associate him with logocentrism; he is therefore unable to understand or counteract the instinctive strength of female bonding. His attempts at control (surveillance by his men, his continual spying, even violence) cannot explain or dissolve their bond; he eventually goes mad and commits suicide.

The motif of the gaze permeates the story in activities such as looking, watching, spying, and gazing. But each activity transcends its visual function and becomes a symbol of power, dominance, affection, or subversion. The women's gaze, which so nonpluses the general, effects a transgressive reordering of dominance. The unique visual bond subverts the patriarchal proprietary gaze, which makes an object of the person viewed; in turn it validates the female gaze, a different, egalitarian mode of looking that negates the binary oppositions of logocentrism.

Moix suggests that the women deploy the gaze as an alternative means of communication that the general cannot decode because it does not take place through normal channels.[8] The women invent a different, disruptive language that conveys meaning through gaps, silences, and the body.[9] Other nonverbal discourse symbolically expands the possibilities for their silent communication: the opera glasses, the portraits that stare at each other, even the "medium" of another female who facilitates a ritual of body language in the exchange of intimate objects.

The women never talk to each other. The general's widow does not speak directly (her speech is always reported and often summarized); even the information she supplies may be untrue. Moix delays the revelation that the narrator of this unusual tale is none other than the unhappy general's son, Rudolph, who, in turn, has had to rely on his father's diaries for most of his data. This convoluted informational chain seems to confirm—ironically—the ultimate power of the male "gaze," because the narrative control is patriarchal: the women's story emerges solely from the limited (and limiting) observations of the two men, who do not allow the women to speak for themselves. The ambiguity in this story thus delays the reader's perception of a biting criticism: an indictment of the patriarchy, personified by the general, who tries to destroy what he cannot understand and in turn, is destroyed by it.[10]

Moix's interest in children's literature and film seems to have prompted her reconsideration of the stock characters and formulaic phrases of these genres. The intertextuality of "Once upon a Time" deconstructs the conventions of fairy tales and stories, imbuing them with a new and unsettling double meaning. Her use of the framework of the fairy tale, combined with metafiction and philosophical questions, creates a stunning form. Characters fruitlessly attempt to edit their unerasable scripts and expose the desperation behind the mask of simple, predictable types from fairy tales (Sleeping Beauty), Spanish children's rhymes (Count Laurel and his widow; the Virgin of the Cave), or popular culture (Disney movies). The linguistic figures (*Once upon a Time, Who He Could Be,* etc.) are even more pathetic: they are immutable forms without substance, whose unhappy protests are equally ineffectual. Literary formulas now reveal a nightmare of predetermined behavior that forces the character (and the reader) to review questions about roles and freedom of action. The repetition of the passage that opens and closes the story (*One Left to Tell It*'s description of his sister) creates a circularity that dramatizes their static existence and the linguistic-textual prison from which they cannot escape.

The juxtaposition of incongruous elements illustrates Moix's postmodern interpretation of the grotesque. Grumpy's fury at

Snow White's suntan or *Once upon a Time*'s quarrels with *Happily Ever After* appear to be humorous rewritings of the usual stuff of children's tales, but desperation lurks close to the surface, and their words are tinged with hopelessness at the "trap of destiny," to quote one of the characters.

"The Naive Man" focuses on the reactions of an increasingly inebriated protagonist as it chronicles his change from smug self-assurance to irrational behavior. The subject for this "study" is an insufferably complacent young man who believes that his keen mind and fastidious habits make him superior to those around him. But as the readers follow the unintentional revelations that describe a downward spiral into offensive drunkenness and the subsequent loss of his "superior" rational faculties, they see that the truth differs considerably from the subject's perception of his condition and environment. The peeling mirror transcends its function as part of the decor by continually supplying the subject—and the reader—irrefutable proof of the distance between self-image and reality.

The interiorized narrative focus allows unmediated access to the ever-degenerating thought processes of the main character. The text carefully reflects this state, sliding from one thought to another without transition, tracking his growing aggressiveness, and transmitting his disbelief at his lack of restraint.

"The Naive Man" is a story of not one but two people out of touch with reality and unable to communicate. The young man is utterly self-assured and egocentric. Unaware of the spectacle he is making of himself, he considers the professor's well-meaning concern for his relationship with Laura to be intrusive. On the other hand, the professor is equally—and erroneously—self-confident in his assumption that the young man understands him. This wordy good Samaritan, who unwittingly illustrates his own philosophy concerning the naiveté of one in love, is as unrealistic as his young table mate. His long-winded oratory and the strained metaphors seem to belie the immediacy of his feelings, making him appear pompous and affected. As in "Once upon a Time," words take precedence over—or substitute for—genuine emotion.

"The Problem" continues Moix's experimentation with the dialectics of mood: she balances a quirky, humorous situation with a tragic question that creates an atmosphere of tension and anxiety. On one level, the fastidious Problem's hubris and his desperate attempts to adjust to the horrid reality to which he is condemned evoke pity. But lest the character become too sympathetic, the writer turns his potentially tragic attempt at suicide into an ironic failure, and the final words mock his dilemma by reformulating a serious existential problem—his self-definition—in terms of a stock situation from popular culture: the one-third remaining Problem is now a media celebrity who insists on unburdening himself in sleazy bars. This final parodic note does not mitigate the gravity of the Problem's search for meaning, which he is unable to find even after an encounter with himself in the mirror.

Like "The Naive Man," this story derives its movement from the interplay of antagonistic concepts. Moix formulates an initial opposition by contrasting the characteristics of a problem (ambiguity, insolubility) with those of humanity (truisms, common sense, sensible thoughts) in terms that are so dramatic and visual that they seem conceived in a cinematic mode.[11] After the Problem arrives at the couple's house, the initial opposition intensifies and recalls a similar contrast in "The Naive Man": the safe, controlled world of abstraction, logic, and reason versus the visceral reactions and sordid behavior of human beings.

The Problem sinks lower and lower from his superior plane: he compromises his lofty standards, finally becoming fond of the couple whose problem he is. Unlike the conceited young man, however, the Problem is a sympathetic character because he is aware of his dilemma and desperately tries to resolve his problem.

The final story is a magnificently developed tone poem of mood change structured around a woman's reactions to a large party that she and her husband are giving to celebrate their fifteenth anniversary. A recurrent visual symbol emphasizes the nightmarish quality of the occasion and of her life: the facing mirror-walls of the living room offer a surreal double reflection of herself and the party, providing a grotesque duplication of reality. Subtle transitions capture the slippage from past to present, from euphoria to anxiety. Recurrent thoughts and phrases provide a textual circularity that emphasizes the protagonist's monotonous life and inability to change, echoing the dilemma of "Once upon a Time" on a more personal level.

The protagonist's alcoholism and depression are in part the result of her "minor role" in the family drama. The guests indirectly make this clear, because they do not see her for her own qualities, but in relation to others—a wife, a mother, the poet's muse. Significantly, she is the only one in the story with no specified name. Like the nameless women in "Dangerous Virtues," she lives in circumstances so delimited by patriarchal values that she has no freedom or autonomy. In this case, her frustration takes the form of alcoholism and depression.

The text drifts off into an anticlimactic open ending, emphasizing the tone of futility. Miguel whispers something unspecified ("words") and receives an unspecified answer ("that neither of them can remember"). These words end the story—and the book—with an action that illustrates the underlying idea of helplessness, estrangement, and the emptiness imperfectly concealed by language.

Moix holds an important place among Spain's women writers, although the rich variety of her production makes it difficult to associate her with a single group. The alienation and critical stance that characterized an earlier generation of women writers (such as Carmen Laforet or Ana María Matute, whom Moix greatly admires) are apparent in her works but transfused with personal, hermetic values that are both autobiographical and generational in nature. Her abiding interest in formal experimentation parallels that evidenced in the literary projects of later writers (for example, Esther Tusquets) who add to their list of accomplishments new techniques, complex narratives, and the demythification of unquestioned national and universal values. Polyphony, subversion, ambiguity, and particularly the primacy of language and text now confirm the unique direction that Moix's work is taking. Her remarkable narrative virtuosity becomes both medium and message as she explores themes that simultaneously reveal her suspicion of the status quo (patriarchal norms, social conformity, literary conventions) and make chinks in its protective armor. *Dangerous Virtues* showcases this remarkable talent; intricate narrative strategies fashion tales replete with unsettling questions, then leave to the readers the task of exploring on their own the spaces opened in the text.

NOTES

1. For an overview of Moix's work, see Margaret E. W. Jones, "Ana María Moix: Literary Structures and the Enigmatic Nature of Reality," *Journal of Spanish Studies—Twentieth Century* 4 (1976): 105–16; Andrew Bush, "Ana María Moix's Silent Calling," in *Women Writers of Contemporary Spain: Exiles in the Homeland,* ed. Joan L. Brown (Newark: University of Delaware Press, 1991); Linda Gould Levine, "Ana María Moix," in *Spanish Women Writers: A Bio-bibliographical Source Book,* ed. Linda Gould Levine, Ellen Engelson Marson, and Gloria Feiman Waldman (Westport CT: Greenwood, 1993).

2. Moix, "Poética," in *Nueve novísimos poetas españoles,* ed. José María Castellet (Barcelona: Barral Editores, 1970), 222.

3. From an interview by Geraldine C. Nichols, *Escribir, espacio propio: Laforet, Matute, Moix, Tusquets, Riera y Roig por sí mismas* (Minneapolis: Institute for the Study of Ideologies and Literature, 1989), 122.

4. Moix, interview by author, April 1996.

5. Two excellent studies of this collection are Linda Gould Levine, "'Behind Enemy Lines': Strategies for Interpreting *Las virtudes peligrosas* of Ana María Moix," in *Nuevos y novísimos: Algunas perspectivas sobre la narrativa española desde la década de los 60,* ed. Ricardo Landeira and Luis T. Gonzalez-del-Valle (Boulder CO: Society of Spanish and Spanish-American Studies, 1987), 97–111 and Bush, "Ana María Moix's Silent Calling."

6. Moix, telephone conversations with author, 1992 and 1995.

7. Levine, "Behind Enemy Lines," offers a perceptive study of this idea, analyzing Moix's "belief that we are all trapped in, men and women alike, by words and texts, that we are all characters of poorly written tales which destroy our autonomy and inner voice" (99).

8. Critics have noted the primacy of language in Moix's work. Bush's overview, "Ana María Moix's Silent Calling," concentrates on the language-silence

duality; Levine, "Behind Enemy Lines," treats the relationship of the characters — and the author — to language and text.

9. This theme echoes ideas on women's language by feminist theoreticians such as Hélène Cixous, Julia Kristeva, and Luce Irigaray. See also Margaret E. W. Jones, "Different Wor(l)ds: Modes of Women's Communication in Spain's *Narrativa femenina*," *Monographic Review/Revista Monográfica* 8(1992): 57–69. When asked about her familiarity with their ideas, Moix stated that she had translated some pieces by Cixous but that at the time she was working on *Las virtudes peligrosas* she had not read these feminists (interview by author, April 1996).

10. This story is so suggestive that it lends itself to many interpretations. In the interview with Nichols, *Escribir, espacio propio,* Moix herself mentions the theme of the double. When asked about bisexuality in the story, she replied, "Esther Tusquets [said that] . . . it was about two women who loved each other very much but never managed to consummate their love. I had not read it that way; in my opinion, it's not even clear that there are two women, maybe only one who is very narcissistic" (114).

11. The execution sequence in "The Problem" is reminiscent of Antonioni's *Passenger* (1975), some of which was filmed in Barcelona.

In the European Women Writers series

The Delta Function
By Rosa Montero
Translated and with an afterword
by Kari Easton and
Yolanda Molina Gavilán

Music from a Blue Well
By Torborg Nedreaas
Translated by Bibbi Lee

Nothing Grows by Moonlight
By Torborg Nedreaas
Translated by Bibbi Lee

Candy Story
By Marie Redonnet
Translated by Alexandra Quinn

Forever Valley
By Marie Redonnet
Translated by Jordan Stump

Hôtel Splendid
By Marie Redonnet
Translated by Jordan Stump

Nevermore
By Marie Redonnet
Translated by Jordan Stump

Rose Mellie Rose
By Marie Redonnet
Translated by Jordan Stump

The Man in the Pulpit
Questions for a Father
By Ruth Rehmann
Translated by Christoph Lohmann
and Pamela Lohmann

Why Is There Salt in the Sea?
By Brigitte Schwaiger
Translated by Sieglinde Lug

The Same Sea As Every Summer
By Esther Tusquets
Translated and with an afterword
by Margaret E. W. Jones